ELLA AT EDEN

For Rebecca McR. Thank you for always pushing me to finish the hike.

Scholastic Australia
An imprint of Scholastic Australia Pty Limited
PO Box 579 Gosford NSW 2250
ABN 11 000 614 577
www.scholastic.com.au

Part of the Scholastic Group
Sydney • Auckland • New York • Toronto • London • Mexico City • New Delhi • Hong Kong • Buenos Aires • Puerto Rico

Published by Scholastic Australia in 2021.

Cover and internal illustrations by Danielle McDonald.
Design by Keisha Galbraith.

A catalogue record for this book is available from the National Library of Australia

ISBN: 978-1-76097-736-8

Typeset in Carniola

Printed by McPherson's Printing Group, Maryborough, VIC.

Scholastic Australia's policy, in association with McPherson's Printing Group, is to use papers that are renewable and made efficiently with wood from responsibly managed sources, so as to minimise its environmental footprint.

The paper in this book is FSC® certified.
FSC® promotes environmentally responsible, socially beneficial and economically viable management of the world's forests.

21 22 23 24 25 / 2

Camp Midnight

LAURA SIEVEKING

A Scholastic Australia book

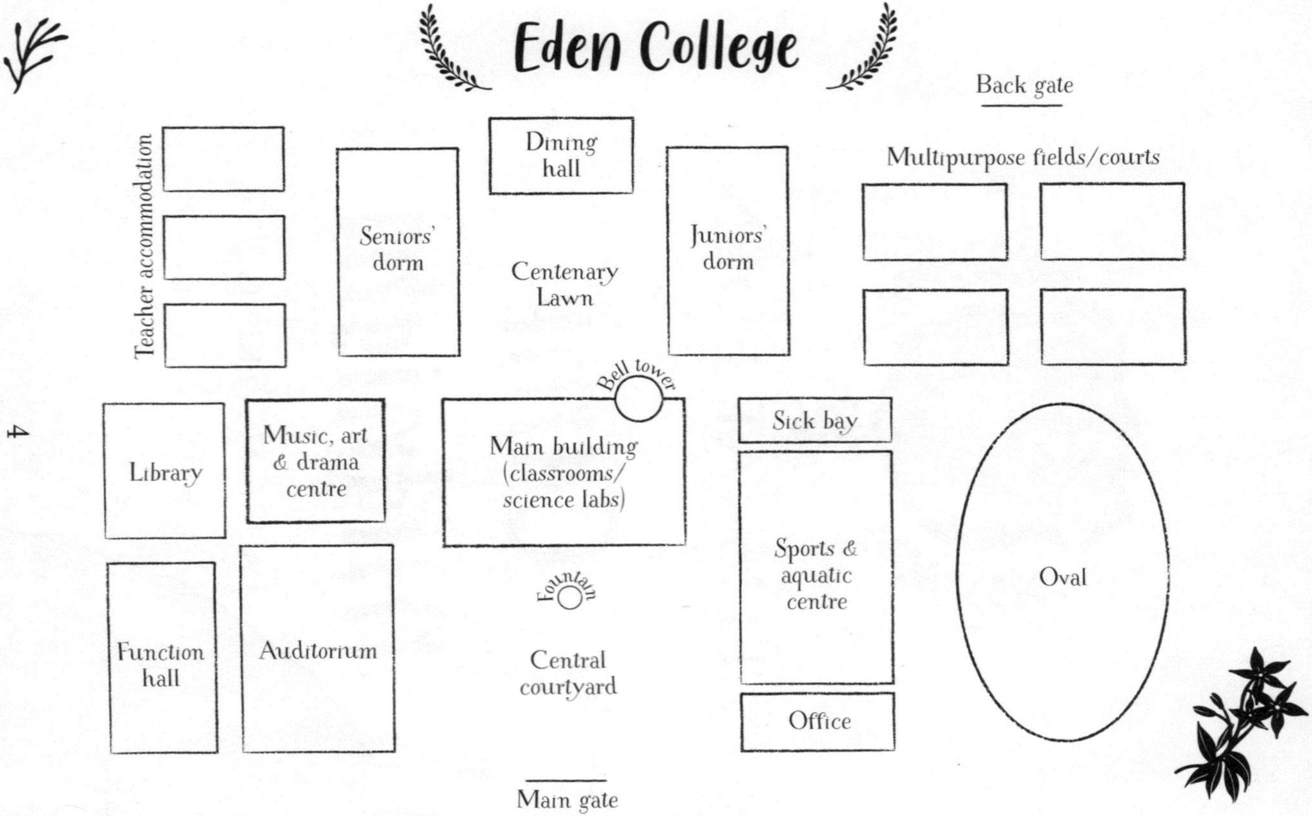

Eden College

Back gate

Teacher accommodation

Seniors' dorm

Dining hall

Centenary Lawn

Juniors' dorm

Multipurpose fields/courts

Bell tower

Library

Music, art & drama centre

Main building (classrooms/ science labs)

Sick bay

Sports & aquatic centre

Oval

Function hall

Auditorium

Fountain

Central courtyard

Office

Main gate

Juniors' Dorm

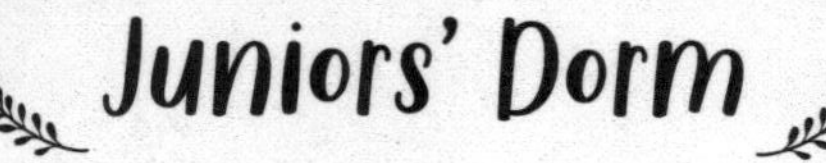

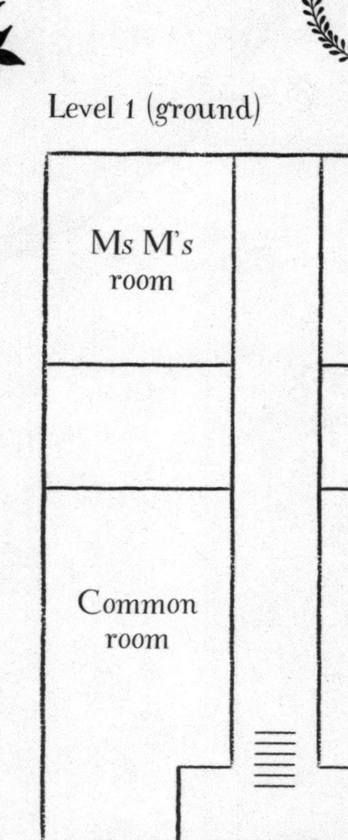

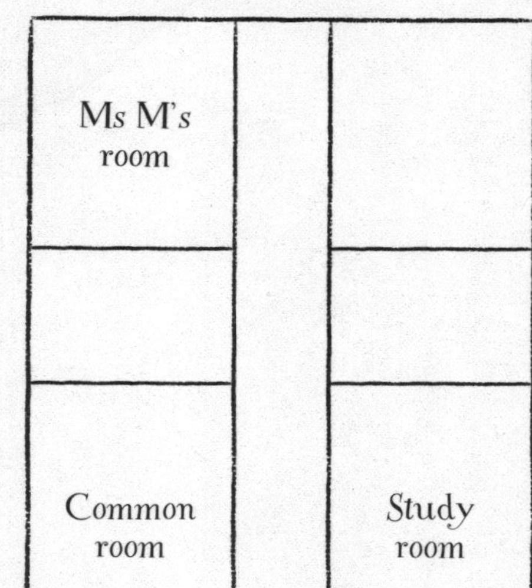

Chapter 1

I looked up the long, dark wooden table. It stretched almost the whole length of the dining room, and was filled with girls from all year groups eating dinner together. The noise echoed around the cavernous room, which had high pitched ceilings. The clanging of pots, plates and cutlery in the kitchen seemed to make the walls vibrate. Boarding school was definitely not the kind of environment you'd want to be in if you didn't like noise. It felt like every day at Eden was noisy. Sometimes I missed the quietness of reading a book in my treehouse back home. Or walking my dog, Bob, to the park in the quiet afternoon sun. Don't get me wrong, I love living at Eden College. But the energy of the school sometimes left me pining for the calm of solitude (which is just a fancy word for being on your own).

I used my knife to saw off a piece of lamb and then I dunked it into my mashed potato. It tasted pretty good and the lamb was nice and tender, but the mashed potato was nothing like Mum's. Mum's mash was always so creamy, and she'd usually add a sprinkling of cheese on the top for an extra bit of flavour.

Splat!

'Ugh, Grace!' I said, exasperated, and rubbed my forehead. 'Stop flicking your peas!'

'Sorry, Ella!' she said from the other side of the long bench table. 'I was trying to get them to land on your plate so I wouldn't have to eat them.' Grace's long dark hair was pulled back in the signature braid she always liked to wear. She was so good at braiding she didn't even need someone to help her with it. Her cat-green eyes shone with mischief as she turned her body slightly and put another pea on the end of her spoon.

She pulled the spoon back like a catapult and flicked it across the table towards Saskia, who was sitting to my left. The pea landed in the sauce on Saskia's plate with a gentle splash, flicking brown droplets onto the front of her uniform.

'Hey, who did that?' Saskia said angrily, looking from left to right.

Grace looked to her other side and pretended to be in a deep conversation with Zoe, who was sitting next to her. Zoe shook her head and muffled a laugh.

'I'll eat your peas! I love peas!' Violet said, holding out her plate to Grace. Violet was sitting beside me, with Grace and Zoe across from us on the other side of the table. Just as Grace was about to dump a pile of peas from her plate onto Violet's, Violet added, 'But you have to take my pumpkin.'

'No deal!' Grace snorted, pulling her plate back towards herself. 'Pumpkin is even worse than peas!'

Grace resumed lining up another unsuspecting victim to receive her next launch of peas.

'Don't forget we've got a meeting after dinner in the

common room,' Zoe said, as she chewed a mouthful of lamb. 'All of Year 7. About camp.'

'Oh, that's right,' Violet said, nodding. 'I almost forgot. I can't believe camp is in just two days!' She pushed her round glasses up her tiny little nose and smiled, but I detected a hint of uncertainty in her eyes.

'I can't wait,' I said, bouncing up and down slightly in my seat. 'We used to go camping all the time back home. We'd go with my twin cousins, Josh and Charlie, and it was so much fun.'

'Ella,' Zoe said evenly, 'remember this isn't camping in a campsite with a toilet block and electricity. This is in the bush. In the middle of nowhere.' Zoe scrunched up her nose and raised one of her eyebrows at me, her deep brown eyes sparkling a little in the dim chandelier light.

'Are you talking about camp?' Saskia interrupted. She put down her knife and fork and flicked her long blonde ponytail over her shoulder. 'My sister, Ivy, said that when she was on Year 7 camp they had to go through some dirty creek and people got leeches on them. LEECHES!'

'Yeah, and my sister said she got gigantic blisters on her heels during the hike and they were so bad that she ended up taking off her boots completely and doing the last bit of the hike in her *bare feet*,' Portia added from next to Saskia.

Portia, Saskia and Mercedes were best friends and did everything together.

Mercedes leaned in from the other side of the table. 'And *my* sister said that when you are putting up your tent, you have to make sure it's not directly under a tree branch, because they have these feral koalas in the bush called drop bears, which drop out of the trees and crush you.' Mercedes' big brown eyes were as wide as saucers.

We all burst out laughing.

Mercedes frowned and shook her head, her thick dark fringe dancing around her face. 'It's true! She saw it on a doctor-mentary.'

'I think you mean *documentary*,' I said, stifling a giggle.

Grace aimed her loaded spoon in the direction of

Ruby and Annabelle, who were sitting towards the front end of the table. She pulled back the spoon and released it, sending a lone pea flying through the air. We watched as it sailed over Ruby's head and plopped with a splash into Ms Montgomery's water glass on the teachers' table. Ms Montgomery, whom we all called 'Monty', was the Vice Headmistress of the school and our Year 7 Coordinator. She was also one of the strictest teachers at Eden College.

We all immediately looked down at our plates, trying not to make eye contact with her. I glanced up and saw Monty stand and look around angrily before shaking her head and sitting back down. We all had to pretend to wipe our faces with our napkins to hide our smothered laughter as she fished the pea out of her water with a teaspoon.

Monty looked back down at her plate and reluctantly started to eat again, clearly cross at not being able to identify the culprit. Her dark hair was, as usual, pulled back in what my Nanna Kate would call a 'severe' bun, which always made her seem even more cross and serious than she probably was. Her beady eyes still darted around the room, looking for anyone with guilt in their eyes.

'I think we'd better go get dessert,' Zoe said.

We all quickly stood and gathered our dinner plates, then shuffled to the rinsing station before lining up for fruit salad.

The common room was alive with the hum of excited and nervous chatter. Words such as 'rafting', 'survival' and 'pit toilet' bounced around the room like bubbles. Some girls reclined on beanbags and others on the couches. Some sat on the floor, sitting cross-legged, anxiously bouncing their knees up and down. The doors opened and Ms Montgomery came in first. As our year level coordinator, it was assumed she would be in charge of the Year 7 camp. She was followed by the Headmistress, Mrs Sinclair, and Coach Bright from the PE department. As always, Coach Bright was dressed in sports gear, her big curly hair in a tumble on the top of her head and pulled back from her face with a retro sweatband, which reminded me of something my Nanna Kate would wear to play tennis.

'Attention, girls,' Ms Montgomery said, as she lightly clapped her hands.

Lots of the girls hadn't noticed the teachers come in and continued chatting, unaware that they had been called to attention.

SQUEEEEEEEEEEEEEEEEEEEEEEEEEEEEEEEEE!

The high-pitched referee's whistle blasted through the air, sounding ten times louder in a tiny lounge compared to out on the sports oval.

Ms Montgomery glared at Coach Bright and mumbled, 'Must you, Janette?'

Coach Bright shrugged, unconcerned.

'As you all know,' Ms Montgomery began, 'camp at Mount Midnight National Park is in just two days.'

The chatter started to rise again and Ms Montgomery frowned. Mrs Sinclair hid a smile behind her hand.

'You've all had your packing lists since before the

beginning of term, so I expect you to have brought everything on the list from home. Please come and see me immediately if there's anything important you do not have, such as a sleeping bag,' Ms Montgomery said.

Saskia raised her hand and Ms Montgomery nodded at her. 'But we don't need our own tents, right?'

'That's right, Saskia,' Ms Montgomery replied. 'You will be supplied with a hiking backpack and one tent between two girls. You will take turns carrying the tent on the hike.'

I looked at my friends. Grace drew a little circle around the four of us, indicating that we should break into two groups and be tent buddies. We all smiled and nodded enthusiastically.

'Part of the aim of this camp is to help you girls get to know each other even better,' Mrs Sinclair said warmly, stepping forward. 'I want you all to consciously try to partner with different people and be brave about choosing new friends.'

Grace winked at us in a silent pact to ignore this piece of advice.

'Use this opportunity to branch out, meet new people! And you might find that surviving three days in the wilderness together helps you get to know someone even better than you know your closest friends!' Mrs Sinclair encouraged.

I looked at Zoe and lightly shook my head. There was no way I could know anybody better than I knew Zoe. We had been best friends for as long as I could remember. We had gone to the same preschool and started school together. We'd been in the same class the whole way through primary school. She knows that my favourite colour is aqua and I know that hers is black and purple (but they have to be together, not on their own). She knows I have a freckle on the inside of my palm and I know she has three freckles in a circle on the outside of her wrist that you can join together with a pen to make it look like she's wearing a watch. She knows I have a little sand-filled toy frog under my pillow, which I squeeze in the night if I have a bad dream. And I know that she always skips the bottom stair in her house because she was sitting on that step when her parents told her that her mum was going to live in another house, away from Zoe and her brother and her dad, and that was the worst feeling in the world. So she decided if she avoided that step every day, then maybe nothing that bad would ever happen again.

Nope, there was nobody I would ever know better than Zoe.

The teachers went through more rules and procedures, which I tried to listen to, but my mind started to wander.

This was going to be my first time camping without my parents. And my first time camping without a campsite. I'd never simply set up a tent in the middle of nowhere before. We were going to have to light our own campfires, cook our own food and dig our own toilet. The whole idea made me jittery with excitement, but also gave me the collywobbles. That's what my Nanna Kate calls the nervous butterflies that flit around your stomach when you are anxious about something.

Mrs Sinclair assured us we would be in the care of professional instructors who knew everything about the bush and would teach us all the survival skills we'd need. But a tiny splinter of worry still lodged itself in my mind.

X –

From: Ella

Sent: Wednesday, 7:02 AM

To: Olivia

Subject: Off to camp!

Hi Olivia!

I know it's early, but I want to send you a quick email before I head off for camp! I'll be back on Friday afternoon. It's only two nights away, but we are not allowed to take our phones so I won't be able to email or call you. Don't worry, I'm going to write down all the funny and exciting things that happen in my notebook so I remember it all, and then I'll video call you when I get back. It'll be like keeping a diary again, the way I did in primary school! And I can also use my notes for an article in the next edition of Eden Press.

I'm super excited but super nervous. I know we used to go camping with Josh and Charlie all the time, but this is not camping at a campsite. This is in the actual bush. With actual wildlife all around us. And actual pit toilets we have to dig ourselves. Yuck, yuck, YUCK! I really hope I won't get bitten by a leech.

Well, time for me to go off the grid, as they say! Wish me luck.

Officially disconnecting,

Ella

xx

I dropped my backpack onto the pavement beside the long white bus. The school had provided hiking packs for us, which were tagged with our names. They were also different colours and designs so we could easily recognise our own. I took an extra look at mine so I'd remember it. Attached to the clips was my sleeping bag, which I'd brought to Eden College from home, as per the camp letter instructions to my parents earlier in the year.

The bus driver was a portly man, and his face glistened with sweat in the morning sun as he flung each bag into the bowels of the bus.

'Do you need some help?' I offered, but he smiled briefly and shook his head before grabbing the next pack and hauling it into the bus cavity.

I lined up at the door of the bus with the other Year 7 girls, waiting to get my name ticked off on Ms Montgomery's clipboard. For the bus journey and the first day's activities, we had been told to wear our school PE uniform with sneakers. We weren't going to be hiking until the second day, and Coach Bright said it's always a good idea to have two pairs of walking shoes in case one got really wet. The morning air was crisp and a breeze gently moved through the yellowing leaves of the trees that lined the long driveway of Eden College. Even though it was likely to get chilly at night on this camping trip, I was sure we would all welcome the coolness of the air when we were on our 20 kilometre overnight hike.

As I thought about the hike, nerves began to bubble up from my stomach into my throat. I shook my head and boarded the bus.

Inside, most girls had already taken their seats and were excitedly chattering away to each other. In our school tracksuits and caps, we all pretty much looked the same. Grace waved to me to come and sit with her. She was halfway down the bus, sitting behind Zoe and Violet. Grace jiggled her legs in her royal blue trackpants and played with the zipper on her blue and teal tracksuit top. She was obviously nervous and excited too.

Once everyone was seated and Monty had gone through the rules *again*, the bus slowly pulled out of the Eden driveway and began to chug up the quiet street.

It wasn't going to be a really long drive as Eden College was already located outside of the major city areas. The national park where we would be camping and hiking was only an hour away.

'Portia, can you braid my hair?' a voice said from the seat across the aisle. Mercedes, with Saskia next to her, was sitting in the seat in front of Portia.

'Of course, Mercedes,' Portia said. She pulled Mercedes' long black hair over the back of her seat and began to brush through it with her fingers.

'Need a brush?' Mercedes asked, reaching into her tracksuit pocket. She pulled out a little travel brush that was folded into a small package.

Portia laughed. 'Trust you to have a brush in your pocket!'

'Need a mirror too?' Mercedes asked, pulling a small foldable mirror out of her other pocket.

Grace and I exchanged glances and began to giggle. Portia looked over at us and smothered a smile.

'My sister says we all need to wear our hair in braids,' Mercedes said loudly to everyone sitting around her.

'Why?' Zoe asked.

'To keep the animals out of our hair,' Mercedes explained.

'I think she meant *insects*, Mercedes,' Saskia quipped.

Mercedes tilted her head to the side, as if thinking hard. After a long pause she said, 'Yes, that *does* make more sense. I was wondering how something like a wombat might get stuck in my hair.'

Portia ran the brush through Mercedes' silky locks. But it snagged each time she pulled it down, catching on something on Mercedes' neck.

'Are you wearing a necklace?' Portia asked.

Mercedes pulled the necklace out from the front of her t-shirt. A beautiful glass pendant hung from a leather string, which was tied at the back of her neck.

'It's my lucky necklace,' Mercedes said, as she twirled the pendant between her fingers. The light bounced around the glass droplet.

'Isn't it a bit precious for a camping trip?' Grace said, scrunching up her nose.

'I got it from an island off Italy where they specialise in glass blowing. I watched the glass blower make it. It's very chic,' Mercedes replied, as if that somehow answered Grace's question.

'How on earth is she going to survive in the wilderness?' Grace whispered to me.

I shrugged. Mercedes reminded me of some girls I went to primary school with. They never liked getting dirty and they always made sure they had immaculate hair. *Immaculate* is a fancy word for perfect. Their lips always had gloss on them, their skin was moisturised and their clothes were flawless. Part of me sometimes wanted to be like them—always looking beautiful. But the other part of me just couldn't be bothered with all that. I mean, don't get me wrong, I love, love, LOVE fashion. For a while I even wanted to be a fashion designer, because I love making outfits match and working out cool colour combinations. But I also like to get out on the soccer field or join in a mud fight—you can't live life like a porcelain doll. At least, that's what my Nanna Kate always says. That's because my Nanna

Kate is an adventurer. She has so many stories about the time she went to the base camp of Mount Everest or hiked Machu Picchu or travelled in a 4WD across the Nullarbor Plain. Nanna Kate always says, 'If you're not living on the edge, you're taking up too much room'. I don't exactly know what that means, but I do know that she loves exploring new places and challenging herself. And I think I've got a bit of Nanna Kate in me.

The bus ambled on until we finally reached a big sign for the Mount Midnight National Park. We all pressed our faces up against the windows, trying to catch a glimpse of the wilderness that would be our home for the next three days.

Piling off the bus, we stretched our legs and breathed in the crisp morning air. Then we gathered around the national park's information centre as the bus driver unloaded our bags from the bus, tossing them into an untidy heap. Ms Montgomery frowned at him as she herded all the girls past the information centre and towards a clearing. Wooden planks had been fashioned into benches that created a semicircle around a big fire pit. Beyond the circle we could see down to the lake, where there was a small jetty and a boathouse with little canoes and stand-up paddleboards propped against it.

'This doesn't look very remote to me. It looks like every other school camp I've been to,' Saskia said, wrinkling her nose.

Even though I loathe Saskia's incessant complaining (that means never-ending whingeing), I had to agree with her. It all seemed a bit too tidy and man-made to be described as 'out in the wilderness', like we'd been told to expect.

'That's because you haven't even begun yet!' a loud voice bellowed behind Saskia, startling us all.

It was Coach Bright, with her usual megaphonic voice. *Megaphonic* means loud and booming. Mum always told Olivia, Max and me that we should have an inside-voice and an outside-voice. Even when outside, Coach Bright's outside-voice was *still* too loud.

'Everyone sit down in the semicircle here,' she instructed. 'This is one of two base camps at Mount

Midnight National Park. This is where you will be taught how to build fires, cook outdoors, make rafts and perform basic first aid. We'll camp here tonight all together, then tomorrow we'll hike up Mount Midnight to the centre of the national park. From there, we will break into groups, with one of the camp instructors helping each group to hike a different route to the end point, which is the second base camp on the other side of the national park. You'll sleep overnight in the bush, without the comforts of a ready-built fire pit and running water from taps.'

Saskia's eyes widened a little. I wondered if she regretted complaining about the facilities at the campsite not being remote enough.

'To start, you need to pair up and come and get your tent with your buddy. We will put up the tents before heading down to the lake for our first outdoor adventure lesson: rafting!' Coach Bright beamed.

I looked over to Zoe and winked at her. I definitely wanted to be with my best friend. It's funny how people can become like a comforting blanket or special toy.

There was a soft bunny that I had had since I was a baby. Now its ears were worn and its nose was no longer pink, most likely from all the kisses I had showered upon it over the years. It was also faded from all the times Mum had been forced to put it through the wash after a night of sickness or being dropped in the dirt on holidays. But my bunny was the thing that always used to help me sleep away from home. It smelt like something familiar—something to hold onto when I felt alone. In many ways, Zoe was like my bunny. She was my little piece of home that made me feel safe in new situations. Sure, our friendship had weathered some tough times, and you might say it was a little pale in colour now and then, but with Zoe I felt safe.

Coach Bright walked over and asked Violet and Zoe to speak with her for a moment. Grace and I exchanged confused glances. Ms Montgomery and Coach Bright had a notebook and were writing things down in it, as well as holding a zipped bag. Coach Bright opened the bag and Violet pulled out different parts of her diabetes medication and instruments for measuring her blood sugar levels. I could also see Coach Bright talking to Zoe, who was nodding seriously.

'What was that all about?' Grace asked, as Violet and Zoe came back over to us.

'Monty needs me to be Violet's buddy,' Zoe said, smiling. 'Just to make sure she's safe and to check on her health as we go along. It means we get to be in the same hiking group!'

'Thanks, Zoe,' Violet whispered warmly.

'So I guess you will need to be tent buddies then,' I said slowly. I felt fear rise up in my chest and catch in my throat.

'That's OK, we can be tent buddies!' Grace chirped, as she linked arms with me. 'And hopefully we are all split into the same hiking group tomorrow, so the four of us can stay together!'

Even though Grace was my one of my roommates, and had been a good friend the whole time I'd been at Eden College, she wasn't like Zoe. She wasn't like my comfort bunny. I forced a smile and tried to look enthusiastic as I nodded at her.

'It'll be fun!' I said in a wavering voice.

Maybe Mrs Sinclair was right. Maybe it *was* time to try and do something outside my comfort zone and without the security of my BFF beside me. I swallowed the feelings of uncertainty and nodded to myself. I could do this.

'Listen up, everybody!' Coach Bright boomed. Ms Montgomery, who was standing next to her, blocked one ear with her finger. 'Come and get your tents and start putting them up in that clearing over there!'

'Do they come with a person to put them up for us?' Mercedes asked.

Everyone laughed.

'What?' she asked, clueless.

'No, Mercedes,' Coach Bright chortled. 'This is your first challenge! TEAMWORK! You and your buddy have to work it out yourselves!'

I looked over to Grace. 'Ever put up a tent before?' I asked hopefully.

'Never!' she beamed. 'But it can't be that hard, right?'

Chapter 3

'Finished!'

I looked across the clearing and saw that Annabelle and Ruby had finished putting up their tent already. Coach Bright went over and inspected it, then declared, 'We have our first completed tent!'

'Grace, we have to get moving,' I said, irritated.

'OK, I think we have everything we need,' Grace said, frowning at the mass of tent poles, little bags and what seemed like an unnecessary amount of slippery material.

'We've been here for 20 minutes and we haven't

even worked out which bit is the bottom,' I said, glancing around at everyone else, who all seemed to be making progress.

Grace smoothed the material out into a basic square shape. 'I think this is the bottom of the tent. Maybe start putting those poles together,' she said, pointing to the pile of black sticks.

I picked up one and noticed it was joined to the others by elastic. The pieces seemed to snap into place, making the pole longer and longer. I thought back to the many times I'd been camping with my family. But it didn't help—tents were never my job. Olivia always loved to put up the tent with Dad. I cursed myself for not ever learning such a basic skill. I was usually on campfire cooking duties with Mum instead. While I might not be able to put a tent up, I *could* make a mean baked bean and cheese toasty over a campfire.

I looked back at Grace, but she seemed to have disappeared.

'Grace?' I asked, looking around.

'In here!' came a muffled reply. A large lump

appeared from under the pile of tent material. 'I thought I might be able to put it up from the *inside*,' she said. 'But now I've lost the door.'

I saw a few of the other girls smother giggles as they pointed to our lumpy, moving tent.

'I think we should try to get the poles in first, so it stands up,' I suggested.

Grace rolled around, trapped inside the tent until she eventually found the zipper door. She crawled out, her hair in a wild tangle and her PE uniform crumpled. Her cap was nowhere to be seen.

'Finished!' I heard Zoe cry out from the area just next to us.

'A little help here then?' Grace said.

'No, no, no!' Coach Bright interrupted. 'This is a skill you need to learn, Grace and Ella! No help from the others. You can work this out if you put your minds to it!'

Grace huffed as we tried to shove the long poles through the loops on the outside of the tent. Slowly, our tent began to take shape. It was starting to actually look like a tent and not just a bundle of dirty washing. Once the tent was standing with the two poles in their correct positions, crossing over the top of the dome, we picked up another large piece of material.

'So what's this then?' I asked.

Grace and I glanced around. Most of the others were at the final stages of putting their tents up.

'Oh, it's a cover to go over the top!' Grace said, pointing to Zoe and Violet's tent.

Grace and I pulled the material over the dome tent, then around and around as we struggled to make the shape of the cover fit the shape of the tent. Finally, like a puzzle piece, it slipped into the correct spot.

Or so we thought.

'How do you get in?' I asked, walking around the tent. The zipper of the cover was open, but it didn't lead to the opening of the tent. It was a door to nowhere.

'We mustn't have lined up the door on the cover with the door on the tent,' Grace moaned.

'Ugh!' I pulled off the cover, irritated.

Everyone else was now unpacking their gear and

changing into their swimsuits for our rafting lesson, which we would be doing after lunch.

Grace and I continued to wrestle with the mass of material that was the cover. Finally, we managed to match the door of the tent cover to the door of the tent. We looked proudly at it. It didn't look too bad!

We crawled inside. It was dim, but seemed roomy enough. I felt the lumps under the tent floor and realised we hadn't cleared away the rocks before setting up the tent. It was going to be an uncomfortable sleep tonight, that was for sure!

'Coach Bright, we're done!' Grace yelled, as we climbed out.

Coach Bright walked over and inspected our tent. Proud of ourselves, we waited for her to declare our tent liveable.

'You've got all the poles in place, and the cover is right,' Coach Bright began, 'but you are missing something.'

Grace and I looked at each other.

'What do you think is in that little bag there?' Coach

Bright asked, pointing to a small sack in the dirt.

Grace opened the bag and tipped out a pile of metal sticks.

'Where do these go?' she asked, frowning.

I picked up one of the metal sticks, which had a curved head at the top.

'Oh, I know what these are,' I said, remembering back to my family camping trips. 'These are the tent pegs. You put them in each corner to stop the tent from—'

But before I could finish my sentence, a gigantic gust of wind whipped through the clearing. Girls shrieked as dust flew up into their faces. Some of the backpacks tipped onto their sides. And with a giant *whoosh*, our tent was blown over and started skittering down the embankment.

'Come back!' Grace yelled, racing down the hill after it.

The tent cartwheeled down, down, down, like a little kid playing roly-poly down a hill.

'Tent! Come baaaaaaaack!' Grace shrieked.

The other girls in our year burst out laughing as Grace and I madly chased after our runaway tent.

'It's heading for the lake!' I gasped.

Grace and I ran faster, but every time we seemed to get close to our tent, it bounced away quicker than before.

'STOP!' Grace shouted at it.

The tent didn't listen.

With a final gust of wind, it lifted off the ground and gently landed in the lake, about ten metres from shore. Grace and I watched, horrified, as our tent slowly filled with water and sank down into the lake.

Grace saluted, like a captain farewelling a sinking ship. 'We had some good times together . . .' she said wistfully.

I gently play-punched her on the arm. 'Grace, this isn't funny, we have nowhere to sleep!'

'Let's go get it then,' she said, shrugging.

'It's full of water! It may have been light when it was dry, but do you know how heavy that thing will be now that it's waterlogged?' I said.

We trudged back up to the supply hut, which was next to the information centre, to tell Ms Montgomery and the campsite staff that we'd lost our tent before we'd even slept in it. My cheeks burned, embarrassed at our incompetence (which is a big word for being really hopeless).

'Well, this isn't a good start, is it?' Ms Montgomery said through narrowed eyes, as she handed us a spare tent that was fortunately available.

I swallowed hard. How were we going to survive the wilderness if we couldn't even get through the first activity?

Monty was right. This was not a good start. And I didn't know it then, but things were only going to get worse.

Much worse.

Chapter 4

Dear Diary,

Wow, it's sooo weird to be writing in a diary again! I want to make sure I remember everything that happens on this trip so I can write an awesome article for Eden Press when I get back to school. But what am I going to write about? Let's see. So far we had a short bus ride to the Mount Midnight National Park. I didn't learn anything new on the way, except that Miranda Richards gets bus sick really, really easily and that she's going to have to use a new hat for this camping trip. I've learned that tent pegs are pretty important, actually. I'd say *essential*, in putting up a tent. And flies are really annoying. I hope that we get to go on an adventure soon, because this is not very interesting material to tell Olivia or for a school newspaper article.

Awaiting adventure,

Ella

I looked at my diary entry and scrunched up my nose. It was really boring. How was I going to write a whole article for Eden Press when I didn't have anything interesting to say? Nobody at school would want to read a recount of camp—that's the kind of thing only *teachers* liked to read. I needed some adventure or mystery, or just anything that didn't involve tent-pitching or hiking. I closed my notebook, thinking I could add to it later. Hopefully I'd have some better material by tonight.

Grace and I had finally finished putting up, and securing, our second tent, and were enjoying a little bit of free time before lunch, which was going to be followed by our afternoon survival lesson on the lake.

For lunch, we gathered around the fire pit, which was not lit at this stage of the day, and enjoyed sandwiches with various fillings to choose from. We also had juice boxes and an ice block for dessert.

As Grace and I sat eating, my face glowed bright red with embarrassment as everyone watched one of the park rangers trying to haul our tent, which was completely waterlogged, out of the lake. He was towing it behind his canoe, and even though we were quite far from the lake, I could tell by his body movements that it was strenuous work. *Strenuous* is a fancy word for when something is super-duper hard work or heavy.

Once we'd helped to clean up after lunch, we all finished getting ready for the afternoon ahead of us. Inside our tent, I slipped on my swimming costume and put my long-sleeved rash vest over the top. We'd been told to bring water shoes as well, which were like little slippers made of wetsuit material. On the bottom they had rubbery patches, which would protect our feet and provide grip on the slippery rocks.

Grace, Zoe, Violet and I walked down to the jetty together, our arms linked. The other girls in our year were lazily sitting on the banks of the lake, soaking in the sun, which was still quite warm despite the ebbing day. There were different types of water activity equipment bursting out of the boathouse, from canoes to paddleboards to kayaks and even small sailing boats.

'Attention, girls!' Coach Bright boomed. 'I'm going to introduce you to two of the Mount Midnight park rangers. This is Andy and this is Martha.'

Andy and Martha were wearing identical khaki uniforms, which consisted of shorts and a buttoned shirt. The Mount Midnight National Park logo was on the chest pocket. Martha's hair was pulled back in a tiny ponytail and Andy's was bundled up in what my Nanna Kate refers to as a 'man bun'. He had a short ginger-coloured beard and a welcoming smile.

'First up, everyone go and get a life jacket from the boathouse,' he said, pointing to a rack on which hung a large supply of life jackets in a range of colours and sizes.

We slipped the jackets on over our rash vests and then gathered back around Martha and Andy for our first activity.

'This afternoon, we are going to have a bit of fun making rafts!' Martha beamed. 'And then later we'll give you a lesson on how to purify water, how to start a campfire and how to cook in the wild.'

An excited murmur rose up from the group.

'Jump into groups of four and we'll get started on the rafts!' Andy said.

Violet, Grace, Zoe and I squealed with delight at the group number being four. Four was perfect for us. There was nothing worse than when teachers told us to get into groups of three. Because four people do not fit into a group of three, and someone would always feel left out.

Martha and Andy led us closer to the lake, where there were piles of wood, barrels and rope all over the ground.

'You need to make a raft out of the supplies you can find here. When everyone is done, we'll have a raft race out around the buoys and back again,' Andy said.

'What elements are important in making a raft?' Martha asked.

'Buoyancy?' Annabelle suggested.

Grace frowned and I whispered, 'It means how much something floats.' Grace nodded and giggled.

'Good knots,' Ruby added.

'Pretty accessories?' Mercedes ventured.

Everyone laughed.

'Yes,' Martha said, nodding. 'Buoyancy is key. You need lightweight materials, otherwise your raft is going to sink. We have empty plastic barrels here, which will float.' She picked up one of the big barrels and tossed it into the lake. Sure enough, it bobbed on the surface of the water. 'Hollow things are good for buoyancy. Like pool noddles, or bamboo and other waterproof natural materials,' Martha continued.

Andy then showed us how to tie proper knots that didn't slip apart. Then we were ready to build.

Grace, Zoe, Violet and I sat down to plan our raft. Zoe, who is always the most logical and organised of the four of us, grabbed a small stick and cleared the ground to make a blank canvas of dirt. We drew our ideas into the cleared space as we debated the best setup for our raft.

'We need enough wood so we can all fit on it sitting down,' Violet said.

'But we don't want too much or it will be too heavy,' Zoe added logically.

Once we all agreed on the most perfect design, we began to gather our supplies. We chose four barrels and only five long pieces of wood for the frame. Four of the pieces would form the outer square of the raft, and one piece would go up the centre for stability. Then we could each sit on a barrel that was secured to the wooden frame with rope.

I glanced over at Saskia. She was in a group with Portia, Mercedes and another girl named Lucy. Their raft design was very different, as they'd chosen to use a lot more wooden planks than us. It meant they had a full surface of wood to sit on and it looked sturdier than our raft with its minimal wood.

'Hey, Grace,' Saskia yelled. 'Want to make a bet?'

Saskia always knew who to approach for a challenge.

'Whichever group beats the other in the raft race has to carry the other's tents on the hike to the summit tomorrow,' Saskia yelled.

'You're on!' Grace said, jumping up.

'Grace,' hissed Violet, 'why do you always drag us into these stupid bets and dares? I don't want to carry their tents!'

'You won't have to,' Grace snorted. 'We're going to smash them!'

Zoe and I exchanged glances and smothered a smile.

As all the groups finished up, Andy and Martha called us to drag our rafts down to the lake for the big race. We were split into a couple of divisions, but Grace and Saskia made sure our two teams were in the same race.

'Grab a paddle each, and then when I say "go", you have to paddle your raft all the way out to the buoy, around it and back to shore. In order to finish, your entire raft needs to be back on land, as well as every member of your team,' Martha explained.

We all nodded and lined up next to our rafts at the edge of the lake. I could feel the cool water gently sinking into my water shoes.

'Ready, set, GO!'

We dragged our raft into the water, and squealed with delight when we saw that it floated. We pushed it out a bit further before jumping on. The plastic barrels were slippery and on her first go, Violet slipped back off into the water. I glanced at Saskia's group, who were able to jump onto their raft much more easily as the whole thing was covered in wood. I winced. Perhaps we'd made the wrong decision in going for as few wooden planks as possible.

Once we were all onboard, we began to paddle. Grace was at the front with Zoe, calling, 'Stroke! Stroke!' We tried our best to keep in rhythm so that we didn't turn the raft.

Saskia's group had a good head start after their fast launch, but we were gaining on them quickly.

'See?' Zoe yelled. 'Our raft is lighter. That's why we are faster!'

Saskia's group were only a metre or two in front of us when they manoeuvred their raft around the buoy.

'My arms are aching!' Mercedes complained.

'Keep going!' Saskia yelled.

As we rounded the buoy behind them, we created some space and dug our paddles into the water hard.

'Stroke! Stroke!' Grace bellowed, willing us to overtake Saskia's raft.

We were now paddling alongside Saskia's group.

'We're too heavy,' Portia moaned.

Our raft pulled out in front and Saskia groaned loudly. I turned and saw her kicking off some of their planks to make them lighter. She pushed four panels off the back, laughing maniacally as she did it. (*Maniacally* means wild and all-over-the-place, like the way my dog, Bob, ripped apart Olivia's pillow and spread the feathers all over the living room that time.)

'That's cheating!' Violet protested.

'No, it isn't!' Saskia retorted.

As Saskia's group's raft became lighter, they gathered speed. We were only ten metres from the water's edge and we were still slightly in front. But Saskia's group hurtled forward with newfound confidence. As we hit the shore, we were neck and neck.

'Pull the raft up!' I yelled.

We hauled our raft up the bank as Saskia's group inched ahead of us. They ran, full speed, over to Andy and Martha and squealed with victory as they crossed the finish line first.

'Losers!' Saskia yelled in our direction.

Grace threw down her paddle angrily.

'We still came second,' Violet said. All the other groups were still either coming up the embankment or paddling into shore, and one group was stranded out by the buoy.

I frowned in frustration as I looked out across the lake to survey the other groups. In the distance, on a high headland overlooking the lake, I suddenly noticed a lonely figure. The person was looking down on the lake through binoculars. I thought it was a woman, as I could see long strands of curly silver hair blowing about her face. Behind her was what looked like a giant dog. I glanced briefly at the other groups pulling their rafts into shore. But when I looked back up to the figure on the clifftop, I realised she'd vanished.

Andy gestured for everyone to gather in around him. 'Congratulations to . . . Ella, Grace, Violet and Zoe! You are the winners of the race!' he yelled.

We looked at each other, puzzled.

'No, *WE* are the winners,' Saskia spat.

'I think you'll find you didn't quite listen,' Martha said, smiling. 'The rule was to finish the race with *all* your group members and *all* the pieces of your raft.' Martha pointed out to the lake where the planks that Saskia had kicked off their raft were floating aimlessly on the water. Martha picked up a paddle and handed it to Saskia. 'Looks like you and your team need to go pick up after yourselves,' she said through a wry smile.

Saskia's cheeks flamed red with anger.

Grace jumped up and down in victory. 'Yes! Winners!' she yelled.

Saskia frowned angrily at us.

'Have fun carrying our tents tomorrow!' Grace teased, as Saskia and her group stomped down the embankment in fury.

Chapter 5

As the sun began to dip low on the horizon, the sky turned pink and orange. The late afternoon breeze had a chill to it, and we all changed into tracksuits, with some girls even wearing beanies on their heads.

Andy and Martha gathered us all together and showed us how to make a campfire. Andy started with some quick-burning leaf litter and smaller sticks and then added larger sticks in a pyramid formation. Once they had caught alight, he asked us to pass him bigger pieces of wood, which would burn for a long period of time. He also took us through all the elements of fire safety that we needed to know.

Even though we were out in the wilderness, we were allowed to use matches to start the fire. But just in case we were ever without matches, or if they somehow got wet, Andy also taught us other clever ways to start a flame, including using Violet's glasses. It was too late in the afternoon to catch a ray of sun through Violet's lenses, but it gave us an idea of how to concentrate the sun's ray into a fine point, which would start a fire.

We all had different jobs to do in order to cook our evening meal. Splitting into groups, some people purified water with tablets, then brought it to the boil over the fire to make rice. Others chopped vegetables, while another group chopped sausages into small pieces to cook like meatballs. But I noticed Saskia, Portia and Mercedes sitting leisurely in a line, braiding each other's hair.

'Aren't you going to help?' I called over to them, as I carried my group's supplies through the campsite.

Portia went to stand up, but Saskia pulled her back down.

'There's nothing more to do, Ella,' Saskia said, gesturing in the direction of all the other busy groups. 'Haven't you heard the saying, "too many cooks spoil the broth?"'

'Are we having broth?' Mercedes asked.

'No, Mercedes, it's just a saying,' Saskia said, rolling her eyes.

'Oh, that's a shame. I love broth. It's so sweet and fluffy,' she said, shrugging.

'Mercedes, a broth is like a clear soup,' Portia said, frowning.

'Oh,' Mercedes said, looking vacantly up to the sky. 'What am I thinking of? The fluffy white meringue with cream and fruit and stuff?'

'That's pavlova!' Saskia hissed, irritated.

Mercedes shrugged again. 'Broth, pavlova. Whatever!'

I decided this wasn't a battle that I could be bothered fighting, so I walked over to Grace, Zoe and Violet. They were collecting metal bowls and trays, as we had volunteered to make dessert. Zoe and I had told the others about a camping trip with my family a couple of years before, where we made brown bears over the fire. Brown bears are basically pieces of cookie dough wrapped around a stick and cooked over the fire, then rolled in melted butter and cinnamon sugar. They are yum, yum, YUM!

We looked through the supplies that I had collected from the campsite staff at the supply hut. The advantage of camping by the supply hut on our first night was that we had access to way more ingredients, as well as a fridge. The following night we would be out in the bush and wouldn't be able to cook with quite so much. So it was time to make the most of it.

Zoe remembered an easy recipe for simple cookie dough, and luckily we had the necessary ingredients available to us. We multiplied the recipe by three, as we knew we would need quite a lot of dough to share around with everyone.

Once we had made the dough mixture, Zoe wrapped it up and put it aside for later. We also put out a bowl of butter ready to melt over the fire and a big metal tray of cinnamon sugar for everyone to roll their bears in when the time came.

With so many people helping out, dinner was soon ready, and we all gathered around the fire to eat our meatballs and rice. And it tasted pretty good!

'So who is on wash-up?' Zoe asked, as she popped the last spoonful of her dinner into her mouth.

'That would be Saskia's group!' Coach Bright bellowed.

'Wait, what?!' Saskia protested.

'You didn't have a task in the meal preparation, so you are on washing up,' Coach Bright declared.

Saskia's face glowed red in the light of the fire, but I think it was glowing more from rage than from the light. I smothered a giggle as Grace, Zoe and I got out our prepared ingredients for the brown bear dessert and Violet melted the butter over the fire.

'OK, so, we are having brown bears for dessert. Ella's family's speciality! Everyone get a long thin stick,' Grace said, pointing to the outskirts of the campsite. 'Then wrap your cookie dough around the stick and toast it over the fire. Once it's cooked, come over here to Violet to brush it with melted butter. Then go over to Ella, who has the tray of cinnamon sugar, and roll your cookie in it!'

Everyone clapped excitedly at the idea of the brown bears, then scrambled to the periphery of the camp area to find the perfect stick. Once everyone had toasted, rolled and tasted their brown bears, they started raving about how good the dessert was.

'Ella, this is amazing!' Annabelle gushed, as she took another bite of her cookie on a stick.

Zoe and I exchanged smiles. Maybe I wasn't so bad at this camping thing after all.

By the time we finished eating our dessert, the sun had well and truly set and the campsite had darkened. We only had the artificial light emanating from the supply hut and the light of the now huge campfire in the middle of the clearing. I zipped up my tracksuit top and pulled a beanie on over my head. It was colder than I had expected after the warmth of the day on the lake.

The teachers and camp staff were having a meeting

in the supply hut, so we were allowed to stay up by the fire for a while. We sang a couple of songs, and told jokes. Then we decided it was time for scary stories.

Portia, who is a great ghost-storyteller, flicked her torch on and held it under her chin so that the light reflected up into her face, making strange and gruesome shadows.

I shivered.

'Many years ago,' she began in a slow, quiet voice, 'this national park was a complete wilderness. There was no supply hut or information centre and no boathouse or jetty on the lake. But there *was* one person who lived here. Her name was Esmerelda Midnight and everybody knew why she lived out here alone.'

'Why did she live out here alone?' Mercedes asked.

'Esmerelda Midnight used to live in a small house on the outskirts of the local town. She was an outcast, and for good reason . . . she was a witch!' Portia said, throwing out her left arm dramatically.

'Yeah, right,' Saskia said, rolling her eyes.

'She was a mean old witch and she hated children,'

Portia continued. 'One day, three children from the town went missing. Everyone knew it had something to do with Esmerelda Midnight, because the last place the children were seen was outside her house, riding their bikes. Now, Esmerelda Midnight's house was plain, with no plants or flowers or anything pretty around it. But right after the three children went missing, three small trees about the size of children suddenly appeared in her front garden.'

'The children?' Violet gasped.

Portia nodded. 'The townsfolk had no way to prove that Esmerelda Midnight had turned the children into trees, but everyone knew it was true. So they banded together to get rid of Esmerelda Midnight. She fled into the wilderness with her large pet dog, who everyone believed to actually be a wolf! As the townsfolk hunted her down, she ran deeper and deeper into the bushland, trying to escape them. But she couldn't lose them. When they finally caught up to her, she cast a spell that made everyone disorientated,' Portia said.

'What's disorientated?' Mercedes interrupted.

'It means lost and confused,' I said quickly, wanting Portia to get back to her story.

'Everyone who had chased her into the bush ended up lost for days, as if they were in a trance and unable to find their way out. But Esmerelda Midnight had not been careful with her spell. When she cast the disorientation spell on everybody, she accidentally struck her wolf-dog with it at the same time. He ran off, confused and dizzy, into the wilderness.'

'Ohhh,' Ruby and Annabelle breathed at the same time.

'Esmerelda Midnight was distraught. Her one companion and friend was gone, and not even her magic could bring him back. Ever since then, she has wandered these trails, calling for her lost pet, wailing for him to come back to her.'

At that moment, a loud 'HOOO!' made us all jump and scream in unison.

'It's just an owl,' Saskia said, shaking her head.

'Or the howl of an eternally lost wolf-dog,' Zoe said with a slight smile.

'And you think the witch is still roaming the national park?' Violet asked Portia, her eyes wide.

Portia nodded solemnly, with one eyebrow slightly raised. 'She roams the Mount Midnight National Park still. You'll recognise her by her long silvery hair and witchy green eyes!'

'Great story, Portia,' Grace said.

'It's completely true. My sister said they spotted Esmerelda Midnight many times on their Year 7 camp here.'

I thought back to the shadowy figure I had seen after rafting this afternoon. A shiver crept up my spine.

'OK, campers,' Coach Bright bellowed as she approached, making us all startle. 'Time for bed. We have a big day tomorrow!'

We let out a communal groan, as we didn't really want to go to bed yet. But we stood up and slowly walked to our tents, with our torches lighting the way.

Grace and I crawled inside, and Grace looped her torch through a piece of elastic hanging from the top of the tent, so it hung down like a chandelier. I smiled at her ingenuity (which is a big word for being clever and inventive).

We changed into our pyjamas and wriggled into our sleeping bags. I could feel the lumps and bumps of the earth underneath the tent and wondered how I would ever get to sleep. Grace reached up and switched off the torch. We lay there silently, listening to the sounds of the night. Suddenly, I heard the faint sound of a dog barking in the distance.

'Grace?' I said, wondering if she was still awake.

'Yeah?' she whispered back.

'Do you think Portia's story is true?' I asked in a slightly shaky voice.

'Oh, Ella,' she laughed. 'She was just making it up.'

'But didn't you see that figure near the lake today? It did look a bit like an old witch. I could see her silver hair blowing in the wind . . .'

'Ella, it's just a story,' Grace reassured me as she yawned.

'Of course,' I said, trying to sound convinced. But as I snuggled deeper into my sleeping bag, I couldn't stop thinking about it. Images of a ragged witch and a howling wolf filled my thoughts. It reminded me of the time that I was scared to sleep over at Nanna Kate's house. I couldn't get to sleep and I crawled out of bed and sat with her on the couch as she wrote in her journal. I had snuggled in under her blanket and she told me that one of the reasons she kept a journal was to help bring out her feelings. She called it 'cathartic', which is a fancy word for that cleansed feeling you get after you've spring-cleaned your bedroom. She tore a page out of her journal and gave me a pen. She told me to think about why I was scared of sleeping at her house and write a story about it. At first, I thought it was just about being away from Mum and Dad, but then I also realised that I didn't like the big grandfather clock in the corridor because it sounded like a monster tiptoeing up the hall. So we wrote a story about a clock monster, which ended up being a very silly story that made me laugh.

That's it!

I sat up suddenly. Maybe I could *write* about the Mount Midnight witch. Sure, it was probably just an old tale, but Portia had said her sister had seen an old lady in the bush too. And all stories come from somewhere. What a great article it would be for the next edition of Eden Press, the school newspaper, if we discovered she was real! *Much* more interesting than a boring recount of our activities at camp.

Grace was already breathing the deep sighs of sleep, so I quietly reached into my backpack and pulled out my torch, along with my notebook. Then I balanced the torch on my knees and began to write.

Chapter 6

The screech of cockatoos woke me with a start. I rubbed my eyes, which felt gritty and tired, and sat up. My sleeping bag slipped down and hung loosely around my middle. The crisp morning air seeped through my thin pyjama shirt. To my left, Grace was still curled up in a ball, snoring lightly.

I reached over to my backpack and pulled out my jumper from the night before. It smelt like old campfire smoke. I wrinkled my nose, but slipped it on over my head anyway. Pulling my sleeping bag off my legs to reveal my long tartan pyjama pants and bed socks,

I crawled on all fours to the opening of the tent, where I'd left my sneakers. I cautiously turned them upside-down and banged each shoe on the sole, making sure there were no creepy-crawlies hiding inside them. Then I slipped them on and exited the tent.

As I stood up, I took in a long deep breath. The air smelt like eucalyptus trees and the smouldering embers of last night's fire. I shuffled over to the campfire area, where a few other girls were sitting, looking just as tired as I felt.

'Good morning,' I mumbled, as I plonked myself on the log next to Ruby and Annabelle. 'Sleep OK?'

Ruby gave a silent nod, but Annabelle grimaced. 'I needed to wee in the night but I was too scared to go outside, so I had to hold it all night long. I was so busting this morning!'

I smiled.

As everyone slowly began to get up, we were given tasks for making breakfast over the campfire. Soon we had scrambled eggs (which were only a little flecked with charcoal), bacon, grilled tomato and fruit salad.

After wash-up, we were told to pack our bags and pull down our tents. Today, we were going to be walking up Mount Midnight, then breaking into groups and getting our overnight hiking routes to the other base camp. The idea was that we would hike for the day and set up camp for the night. But this wasn't like sleeping in our tents at the campsite, oh no, it wasn't. This was proper camping in the middle of nowhere. We would have to find a good place to stop and create our own campsite. There'd be no campfire already set up. No supply hut with spare supplies. We would eat what we carried. And we would have to wee . . . in the bush.

'How is this possible?' Grace moaned, as she dropped our tent bag to the ground. 'Did our tent grow in the night?'

I looked over at her and smiled. She was trying to fit the tent back into its bag, but, for some reason, the bag was bulging full even though half the tent was still overflowing out the top. I scratched my head and looked around. The others seemed to have been able to fit their tents back into their bags with ease, and were busy strapping them onto their hiking packs.

'At least we don't have to carry the tent,' I said. 'That's Saskia's team's job after our raft race win!'

Grace didn't smile. She was too focused on trying to wrangle the tent into the bag.

I helped her pull the tent back out and we tried to refold it along the creases it still had from when we'd first pulled it out of the bag yesterday. Then we tried again to stuff it back into the impossibly small bag.

'I swear tents are our nemesis,' I grumbled.

'Neme-what?' Grace said.

'Nemesis. It means your mortal enemy,' I said, as I tried to make sure there was no air between the folds of the tent material.

'I don't care what the official word is. I'm just going to call it a big pain in the bu—'

'Ready?' Zoe and Violet interrupted. They had successfully packed up their tent and supplies already.

'A little help?' I asked.

Zoe shook her head and started folding our tent all over again. I felt like a little kid who couldn't do up their shoelaces by themselves. Completely useless.

'Let's hope we are in the same group so I can help you two out,' Zoe laughed.

I frowned. I knew she was just joking, but I didn't like the idea that I couldn't look after myself.

Coach Bright called everyone over to the campfire area so that we could talk about how the day was going to run. We all gathered on the logs, hot from packing and still a bit bleary-eyed from our interrupted sleep.

'Girls, today we are going to hike to the summit of Mount Midnight. Once we get there, we are going to break into groups and each group will be assigned a ranger from the Mount Midnight National Park.' Coach Bright gestured to a group of people wearing the national park's uniform. I recognised Andy and Martha from rafting yesterday, but the others were new to me. They all wore solid hiking books and looked very . . . outdoorsy.

'The rangers will help everyone in their group improve their survival skills, and I expect you all to be on your best behaviour. Each group will be given a different route, and you will all use a map and the survival skills you have been taught to camp overnight in the bush tonight and make your way to the final base camp tomorrow,' Coach Bright boomed excitedly.

Nervous butterflies flittered around inside my stomach. *It's OK*, I told myself. *We are with qualified park rangers. We will be fine.*

'Grab your gear, and let's go!' Coach Bright yelled.

I picked up my backpack, which seemed to weigh a lot more now that it had food supplies in it as well as my sleeping bag strapped to the top. I frowned and tried to adjust the shoulder pads so they were more comfortable. I wasn't sure how my shoulders would be able to cope carrying this weight all day.

'Use your straps, Ella,' Zoe said, walking over to me. She clipped the waist straps together and pulled them tight. I could already feel the weight shifting from my shoulders to my midsection.

'Now tighten this,' Zoe said, clipping the smaller strap across my chest. She pulled the shoulder straps tighter and the whole pack seemed to lighten as the weight distributed itself across my torso.

'What would you do without me?' she winked.

I smiled at her in thanks, but then frowned slightly as she turned way. What *would* I do without Zoe?

Grace wandered over to where Saskia, Mercedes, Portia and Lucy were standing. I could see she took great joy in handing our tent over to Saskia. Zoe handed her and Violet's tent to Portia.

'Enjoy the hike,' Grace said in a mocking voice.

Saskia rolled her eyes.

We followed the park rangers out of the campsite and onto the hiking trail. The trail was quite wide so we could walk four abreast without a problem. I knew it would get steeper and narrower as we went, so I was happy for the mild incline and the chance to chat and walk at the same time.

'I spy with my little eye, something beginning with G,' Grace said.

'Grace?' I said.

'Garden?' Zoe ventured.

'Grass,' Saskia said, joining in.

'Giraffe?' Mercedes offered.

'Giraffe?!' we all shrieked.

'What? Giraffe starts with G, right? Or is it J?' Mercedes mused.

'You have to be able to *see* it, Mercedes. Haven't you ever played I Spy?' Portia said, shaking her head.

'Oh. Is that why it's called I *Spy*? I always wondered about that,' Mercedes replied, shrugging.

As the trail narrowed and became steeper, we filed into a single line and talked less. I noticed my breaths becoming more laboured and my calves beginning to tighten. I knew I'd have sore legs tomorrow!

The sun peeked through the trees and the dry leaves crunched underfoot. Some of the tree trunks had streaks of black from the bushfires that had torn through the park several years before.

The girls ahead of me suddenly stopped. They were whispering excitedly and pointing. I walked up to them and craned my neck to see through the bodies, trying to catch a glimpse of what they were looking at.

Martha was up the front, gently waving for everyone

to gather around her, while keeping her finger up to her lips, silently instructing us to keep quiet.

That's when I saw it.

In the middle of the path was an echidna. It was slowly ambling across the trail, its brown spines majestically splayed behind it. Its long narrow nose sniffed the ground, looking for insects as it waddled along.

'Everyone, keep very quiet!' Martha whispered.

'Is it dangerous?' one of the girls asked softly, eyeing the echidna's spines.

'No, not if we respect it,' Martha smiled. 'He's just going along his way and if we let him continue to go where he wants to go, he's not going to pay too much attention to us. That's the thing with our local wildlife—most of the time they have no interest in humans. It's only when we startle them that they feel the need to defend themselves.'

I nodded as we watched the echidna continue into the bushland. Once it was gone, we all exhaled as one and started chattering about how exciting it was to see an echidna in the wild.

We continued our hike up, up, up the trail, until we finally broke free from the scrub and out onto a lookout. It was only after I'd thrown down my pack and had a long drink from my water bottle that I really took in the scene before us. I joined the other girls and we all stood silently, in awe.

We could see right across the national park, and the bushland below us dropped off sharply. I couldn't believe we had climbed so high! The expanse of trees in front of us was brown, green and yellow, in all the rustic hues of the Australian bush.

'If you look down to the bottom there,' Martha said, pointing right to the base of the canyon, 'you can see the river, which flows the whole way through the national park. If you follow it to the right, it leads to the lake you were rafting on yesterday. And if you follow it to the left, you'll see it leads to the opposite side of the park, right to the base camp you are hiking towards today and tomorrow.'

'Wow, that's a long way,' Violet breathed in my ear.

I nodded.

'We'll take a lunch break here, then split into groups, check each group has enough gear and give you your routes to hike. There are various ways to the end point, so we will be testing your orienteering skills by having you follow different trails,' Martha explained.

I gulped.

'But don't worry,' Martha said, sensing our apprehension. 'Each group will have a park ranger to guide them, so you'll be just fine.'

After we'd sat at the lookout for some time, taking in the sheer magnificence of the scene, we moved into groups to eat lunch. We had packed fruit and wraps and other bits and pieces to make a hearty meal before what we all expected would be a long afternoon of hiking. As we ate, Coach Bright passed around a clipboard which had a list of the groups for the hike and overnight stay in the bush before finishing at the end point the next day. I desperately wanted to be with Zoe, and Grace and Violet too.

'Let's see,' Saskia said, snatching the clipboard from

Grace. 'Ugh, I'm with *none* of my friends. This isn't fair!' She threw the clipboard to the ground.

I picked it up and hurriedly scanned the first list. I immediately saw Zoe and Violet were together. It made sense because Zoe was Violet's buddy for the trip. And they were in a group with Coach Bright and Martha, who were probably the most experienced adults there. I figured it was because they needed to watch Violet's diabetes. But Grace and I weren't in their group. I felt my chest tighten.

Each group was on a separate page, so I flipped ahead, quickly scanned another group and saw Grace's name. But I wasn't in her group either. I heard her grumble as she looked over my shoulder.

All I could hope for now was to be in a group with some of our other friends, like Ruby or Annabelle.

I finally found the group I was in, and scanned the names—names of girls I was in classes with and one girl from Eden Press.

But none of my friends were there.

My breathing quickened and I felt a bit sick.

No Grace. No Zoe. No Violet. Not even Ruby or Annabelle.

I was all alone.

Chapter 7

I couldn't finish the rest of my lunch. It felt like I had swallowed a stone. I walked silently to the lookout and gazed at the bushland below. It wasn't fair. I picked up a small rock and threw it angrily over the clifftop. Camp was supposed to be one of the most fun things we did all year. And now I wasn't even going to be with my friends.

It reminded me of the time when my Nanna Kate was supposed to take me on a special holiday for my tenth birthday—just the two of us, because I was turning double digits. And then I got chicken pox.

I had to lie in bed and watch boring daytime television while Olivia and Max went to the movies and putt-putt golf and even the zoo without me.

But then I remembered what Nanna Kate did next. She'd said if she couldn't take me on holidays, then she'd bring the holidays to me. She came over and set up the garden with decorations. She made me a high tea and we sat in the yard in our best dresses, sipping tea and eating scones. Nanna Kate always said that your attitude was the thing that would make or break an experience. Maybe she was right. I exhaled slowly and looked back over to where the other girls were all sitting, laughing and eating the last bits of their lunch. Maybe it would be a good opportunity for me to be a bit more independent. Maybe I *could* learn to survive without the safety of Zoe.

Suddenly, a movement across the valley caught my eye. On one of the other cliff edges, not too far from my own lookout, I saw something glint in the sunlight. I moved my head and squinted. It was a person. I gulped and tried to bring them into focus.

The figure was looking through binoculars. And they were pointed directly at . . . me. I startled. They lowered the binoculars. Then a gust of wind picked up, and the person's hair splayed out from behind her. Long silvery strands of hair . . .

'I saw your name. Rubbish group—how unlucky.'

I jumped and turned to see Saskia standing behind me. I rolled my eyes. I was not in the mood for her drama. I looked back to the cliff face, trying to find the figure again, but she had disappeared.

I shivered.

'You know, I'm in a pretty bad group too,' Saskia sighed. 'And so is Mercedes. It's like they decided to make all our lives hell out here.'

I shrugged. 'Maybe they just want to challenge us a bit.'

Saskia laughed mockingly. 'Sometimes you have to take matters into your own hands,' she said in a silky, purring voice.

I narrowed my eyes. What was she up to?

Saskia pulled something out from behind her back.

It was the clipboard with the group lists on it. She flicked from one page to the next, running her finger down the lists.

'Ooh, *this* is a good group,' she said, pointing to one of them.

'Saskia, there's nothing we can do about it. The groups are set,' I said, resisting the temptation to trawl through the list of names for a second time.

'Well, it can't be *that* set in stone. They didn't even use a pen!' she laughed.

I leaned over and looked. Sure enough, the lists were written in pencil.

I shrugged again. 'So?'

Saskia reached into her pocked and pulled out a pencil. It had the small nub of an old eraser on the top of it.

'Look here,' she said, pointing to the top of the first list. 'It says which instructors are with each group. The only group with a teacher from Eden College is Coach Bright's group. Monty is meeting us at the end. The other groups are all led by park rangers—they don't know who we are.'

I looked into her piercing blue eyes, which shone at the prospect of mischief.

'I—I'm fine with my group,' I stammered. 'Grace is in a group without her friends too, and she's fine.'

'She didn't *sound* very fine,' Saskia said. 'She sounded pretty annoyed actually. Just like me . . .'

Saskia flicked through the pages of the groups again, finally stopping on another one. She pointed the pencil eraser at the page and dragged it down until she stopped on a name. I looked over her arm to see what she was pointing at.

'All we have to do is . . .' And she rubbed out her name from the list.

'Mercedes wants a different group too,' she said, flicking to the next page. 'Ha! She's right above Grace! I can just delete them both,' Saskia said, erasing the pencil markings.

'Saskia,' I said, looking around to make sure no teachers were watching, 'they are going to notice all the rubbed-out marks on the page.'

'Hardly! The rangers will just think the teachers were shuffling around the groups last night in their meeting. There are rubbed-out names all over this thing. Besides, the groups are all different sizes, so no one will notice if some have more girls than others.' Saskia was always so self-assured. 'And here you are, Ella. Do you want to do the honours?'

She held out the clipboard and pencil in my direction. I put my hand out to take them, but hesitated. I didn't want to get into trouble.

'I've already rubbed Grace off. You can just write your names back into the same group, so at least you'd be together!' she said. 'Or maybe join Ruby and Annabelle.'

I looked back over at the girls and saw Zoe and Violet laughing together, while Grace scowled.

It wouldn't hurt, would it?

I quickly took the clipboard and rubbed out my name from the list. Then I flicked through the remaining groups to see which one I should add Grace and my names to. I knew we couldn't be with Violet and Zoe in

Coach Bright's group, but there was another group with Ruby and Annabelle that *did* look fun. I hovered the pencil over the page, but just as I went to start writing, a loud voice made me jump.

'Oh, *there's* my clipboard!' Coach Bright boomed, walking over to Saskia and I at great speed.

I hurriedly closed the pages so the first list was showing again.

'Did you find your groups?' Coach Bright asked, taking the clipboard and turning the pages.

'Yes, we did!' Saskia and I yelled at the same time, hoping to distract Coach Bright from noticing the rubbed-out pencil marks where our names used to be.

'Good then! Get ready, campers! We'll be dividing into our groups soon!' Coach Bright turned with her clipboard and walked away.

'Great! Now what do we do?' I hissed at Saskia. 'You, me, Grace and Mercedes aren't on *any* lists. Now we are sure to get busted and it's all your fault!'

Saskia rolled her eyes. 'Calm down, Ella. It's *fine*. Once the groups are formed, we can easily just join a group and tell the ranger we were swapped into it by Coach Bright. What is the ranger going to do? Send us away on our own in the middle of nowhere?'

I chill whipped up my spine. *On my own in the middle of nowhere?!*

'I guess,' I said uncertainly.

'You'd better go tell Grace the plan,' she said, as she skipped over to Mercedes, beckoning her to go with her for a 'secret chat'.

My legs felt a little shaky as I slowly walked away from the lookout, back to the group. Maybe Saskia was right. The park rangers would have no idea who was in which group. As long as we were in *a* group, no harm had been done, right?

I swallowed hard, suddenly unsure.

Chapter 8

Coach Bright read out the group names and the rangers who were going to lead each group. Saskia, Grace, Mercedes and I shuffled nervously, hoping nobody would notice that we hadn't been put in a group. I'd sheepishly told Grace about the incident with the lists, hoping she wouldn't be mad. She wasn't—she'd thought it was a great idea. But we hadn't told Violet and Zoe. Thankfully they were too busy talking to their own group to worry about Grace and me.

'Final toilet stop!' Coach Bright hollered, and lots of girls wandered into the bush to find a quiet secluded place to do a wee. Gross, gross, GROSS!

I pulled my pack onto my back and tightened the straps as Zoe had showed me earlier that day. Then I leaned over to Saskia.

'We still haven't put ourselves on a list,' I hissed into her ear.

'It's fine,' she answered, waving her hand. 'Just join the back of Ruby and Annabelle's group. Mercedes and I will jump in with Portia. Then once we set off, you can tell the ranger that you were swapped into the group. Crisis over.'

I frowned. Was it really that simple?

Mercedes wandered over with her hiking pack strapped on tightly.

'Is the line for the toilet long?' she asked Saskia.

Saskia rolled her eyes. 'What toilet, Mercedes? There *is* no toilet.'

'Oh,' Mercedes said, puzzled. 'I thought that's what Coach Bright meant. That there was a toilet block somewhere out here . . . in the wilderness . . .'

'Just go find a tree to pee behind,' Saskia said,

sounding irritated.

'I'll show you where to go,' Grace said. 'I need to go too.'

Mercedes and Grace walked off into the scrub, with Mercedes shrieking the whole way as twigs and branches clawed at her legs and arms.

'Line up, campers!' Coach Bright yelled.

'They'd better hurry,' I said nervously to Saskia.

The groups slowly formed and the rangers started marking their rolls.

I jittered my legs, nervous about the idea of joining a group I wasn't meant to be in. Maybe this was the time to come clean and just go with my original group. I bit my lip nervously.

'I wish the others would hurry up,' I said, craning to look into the dense scrub where Grace and Mercedes had disappeared.

'Oh, come on, worry wart,' Saskia said, grabbing my arm and pulling me into the bush. 'We'll find them and tell them we're leaving!'

Saskia pulled me along, bashing a path through the

scrub with a long stick she had picked up.

'Mercedes! Grace!' she yelled.

The dry leaves crackled underneath my feet as we stomped through the dense undergrowth, calling our friends. Finally, we heard the faint voices of girls.

'What are you two up—' I started to say, but didn't finish my sentence as we broke through the thick bush and into an open area . . . which dropped steeply and unexpectedly off a cliff!

Grace was peering over the edge, looking worried.

'What are you doing?' Saskia yelled. 'Get away from the cliff, Grace! Where's Mercedes?!'

'She's down there!' Grace said with wide panicked eyes, pointing over the edge.

Saskia and I shuffled closer to the drop-off and looked over. There was Mercedes, on a narrow ledge below us. She was just standing there, looking up at us. She seemed rather calm considering she was on quite a thin ledge hovering over a massive drop into the canyon below. The word that jumped into my head was 'jeopardous'. Which means very dangerous.

'Oh my goodness, what are you doing?' I shrieked.

'I put my pack down and went to go to the toilet behind that tree. Turns out behind that tree is a cliff!' she said in a sing-song voice. Mercedes was either incredibly brave or just really clueless as to how much danger she was in.

Grace was now lying on her tummy, trying to reach Mercedes with a long branch.

'I thought I'd be able to pull her up, but this branch is too short,' she said, kneeling up and tossing the branch to the side.

'We need a rope,' I said, looking around us.

'Does anyone have rope in their bag? Maybe from their tent or something?' Grace asked wildly.

Saskia shook her head. Her cool demeanour had disappeared and she looked scared and worried.

'Oh, like a skipping rope?' Mercedes asked from over the edge.

'Well, yes, but we don't have one of those!' Grace said, exasperated.

'I do!' Mercedes called back. 'It's in my pack.

It's part of my fitness regime. I do 200 skips every day to keep me healthy!' she said.

We all looked at each other, disbelieving. Who brought a *skipping rope* on a camping trip?!

Saskia rushed to where Mercedes had dumped her hiking pack and pulled out a long pink skipping rope from the front pocket.

'We need to make sure it's anchored,' Grace said, tying the rope to the thick tree closest to the edge of the cliff.

'Tie it tight,' Saskia instructed.

I stood to the side, trembling. I felt completely useless as Saskia and Grace worked together to secure the rope.

'What can I do?' I stammered.

'Just keep clear,' Saskia said, shooing me out of the way.

My chest felt tight. There was a disaster and I was no help at all. This was exactly what Zoe was talking about earlier. What *would* I do without my friends saving the day? I felt redundant. Superfluous. Expendable.

Which are all just big words for completely useless.

'Now, Mercedes, wind the rope around your wrist and then use it to help climb up,' Saskia said.

Mercedes calmly looped the rope over her wrist. Then she pulled on it as she coolly walked her feet up the steep incline of the cliff. When she got close to the top, Grace and Saskia, who were lying on the ground on their stomachs, reached forward and grabbed the waistband of her hiking pants. With a final pull, Mercedes tumbled over the top of the ledge, back onto safe ground. Saskia, Grace and Mercedes lay on the ground for a few seconds, panting. Then Mercedes burst out laughing.

Grace caught the giggles and then Saskia joined in too. They lay there, laughing hysterically, while I stood watching on.

'Um, I don't think that was very funny,' I finally said.

They slowly rose to their feet.

'You're right,' Grace said, wiping tears from her eyes. 'I think that was more relief than anything else.'

We all picked up our hiking packs and moved well

clear of the cliff face before throwing them over our shoulders.

'We'd better get back,' I said nervously. 'Coach Bright is going to be looking for us everywhere. She's going to lose it when we come back so late.'

Grace and Saskia nodded.

'We're *fine,*' Mercedes laughed. 'Silly Ella.' She laughed again.

We all stopped and turned to look at her.

'What's so funny?' I asked.

'Don't worry, Coach Bright isn't looking for us. We're not on any of the lists! *Nobody* is looking for us, so we won't be in any trouble!' Mercedes said happily.

Panic filled my chest as horror washed over me. I looked at Grace—her face had gone completely pale. Saskia's eyes were wide.

'Quick!' Saskia yelled, as she started to bolt back through the scrub.

We followed each other in single file, using our arms to bash through the dense bushland.

'Come on,' Grace huffed. 'Quickly!'

My calves ached as I scrambled up the incline of the hill, with my heavy pack seemingly pulling me backwards with each step.

'Why are we running?' Mercedes yelled from the back.

We finally broke out into the clearing where the rest of our year had been gathered in their groups. I looked around wildly.

'Hellooooo!' Grace hollered. 'Anybodyyyyy?!'

'Coach Briiiiiight!' Saskia yelled. But she was met with complete silence.

We were in the bush.

All alone.

And nobody knew we were missing.

Chapter 9

There was a bull ant pulling a cockroach along the bumpy grey rock I was sitting on. The roach was ten times the size of the bull ant, but that didn't seem to deter it. I stared as it dragged the roach along the surface of the rock and then down onto the dirt below. It disappeared under the leaf litter.

'Ella? Hello?' Grace nudged me and I startled.

'OK, so now that we are *all* listening, what are our options?' Saskia said, picking up a stick and clearing the leaves from a square of dirt to form a blank canvas. She pointed the sharp end into the dirt and wrote:

1. Stay put.

'They always say that if you are lost, you should stay where you are and wait for help to come to you,' she said.

'But that's only if someone is trying to find you. Nobody knows we are missing. And they are not going to notice we are missing until they get to the base camp on the other side of the national park . . . tomorrow!' I said, tears pricking my eyes. 'I can't believe I went along with your plan, Saskia. I *knew* it was a bad idea!'

'You seemed fine with it when you were going to be with a better group!' Saskia spat.

'Guys, chill,' Grace said, shaking her head. 'Back to the plans. What else can we do?'

Saskia glared at me, then picked up her stick again. She wrote the next option in the dirt:

2. Try to find help.

We looked around silently. The only thing we could hear were the sounds of the bush—cicadas, the crackle of the wind through the dry leaf litter and the mocking laughter of a kookaburra.

'Anybody sneak a phone on the trip?' Grace asked hopefully.

We all turned to Mercedes.

'Don't look at me! I didn't bring mine. I didn't want to smash my new screen!'

'Well, then there's only one option left,' Saskia said matter-of-factly, writing a third option in the dirt:

3. Hike to the base camp.

We all looked at each other, assessing each other's reactions.

'It's not that hard,' Saskia said. 'Look . . .' She got up and led us all to the lookout. 'See down there? That's the river. Martha said the river flows all the way to the other side of the national park. That's our end point. That's where everyone is going.'

'But we don't even have a map,' I said, my voice shaking a little.

'Saskia's right—we won't need a map,' Grace said. 'If we follow the trail down to the river, we can follow the river right to the end. This is a national park with established walking trails. I think we'll be fine.'

I nodded uncertainly. 'Do we go to the end point or back to the beginning?'

'I think the end point is more sensible,' Grace said. 'That's where everyone else is going. If we hike back to the start, there's no guarantee there will be anyone there. We could be stuck there without communication, especially if the information centre and supply hut are locked up.'

Saskia nodded in agreement. 'Grace is right. Our best bet is to catch up to the others.'

'Do you think we should try to leave clues, in case someone *does* try to find us?' I asked.

'Like what?' Saskia said.

'Markings on trees or something—anything that points to where we are going. Just in case they somehow work out we are missing and come looking.'

'Good idea,' Grace said. 'We could try and make some bush paint. Like, we could mix dirt with water and . . .' Grace's voice trailed off. Bush paint wasn't going to be very visible.

We all turned to Mercedes, who was sitting quietly.

She had her compact mirror open and was applying a shimmery red lipstick to her lips.

'You brought *lipstick*?!' Grace laughed.

'It's hydrating lip shimmer. Nobody likes chapped lips, Grace.' Mercedes rolled her eyes.

'It's perfect!' Saskia said, snatching the lipstick from Mercedes. She walked up to a tree by the trail and drew a bold, shimmering red arrow pointing down the trail for the river.

Mercedes squealed, 'What are you doing? That lipstick is from FRANCE!'

As we walked down the trail, I could feel the descent in my thighs and calves. It felt like I was being pushed forwards, about to fall, as my heavy pack prodded me downhill. Every now and then we'd stop at an obvious landmark, like a protruding boulder or a conspicuous tree, and we'd draw a big lipstick arrow pointing down the hill. The bushland around us was thick and the trail was narrow. The ground underfoot seemed less dry than at the lookout. I looked up and a thick canopy of leaves sheltered us from the sun. The air smelt cool and a little dank in this thicker part of the bush. My eyes darted from left to right, checking for unfamiliar insects and wildlife. I couldn't help but think back to what Portia had said about leeches on her sister's camp. I never, ever wanted to get bitten by a leech. Olivia got one in her sock when we were camping once and it was yuck, yuck, YUCK!

As we trudged on, the sound of running water became louder and louder. We knew we were getting closer to the river, which would be our map out of the national park. When we reached the bottom of the hill, the trail flattened out and we found ourselves walking on a proper dirt path. The sun began to peek through the canopy, which became sparser as the bush became less dense. The trickle of a stream started to sound more like the rush of a river. Suddenly, we stepped through a line of trees and found ourselves in an open clearing facing the wide flowing river of Mount Midnight National Park. It rushed along, much faster than I had been expecting it to flow.

We looked around. It was like we were standing on a tiny flat beach, but instead of sand there was dark dirt underneath our feet. To our left was a towering wall of rocks. To our right was thick dense bush. And in front of us was the gushing river. There was a small sign saying, 'Valley Cove'.

'Wait, what?!' Saskia exclaimed, as she threw down her pack. 'Why has the trail led us to a dead end?!'

We all looked at each other and shrugged.

'Maybe this trail isn't meant to keep going. Maybe it just leads here . . .' Grace's voice trailed off.

We'd been hiking down the mountain for hours. There was no way we had the time, the drinking water or the energy to hike back up to the lookout and start again.

'This is why we needed a map!' I yelled, folding my arms across my chest.

Grace cupped her hands above her eyes to block out the sun and tried to see across the river.

'I'm pretty sure the trail follows the river on the other

side,' she said, craning her neck to look downstream.

'We can't swim over,' Saskia said. 'We have packs and we don't want them to get wet. Or our food.'

'Or our *hair*,' Mercedes added, aghast.

I gazed at the river. A light branch was floating on the surface, being carried along at a good pace. Just like a little speedboat.

I started to look around the riverbank, stopping and picking up bits and pieces of debris that had become caught in the cove. Mercedes looked at me and scrunched up her nose.

'So much junk,' she said, kicking aside an aluminium can. 'People are gross.'

I tiptoed over the rocks at the edge of the river and glanced around the embankment.

'Guys! Look!' I yelled.

The others came stumbling over the rocks.

'What am I looking at?' Saskia asked.

'That big crate!' I said.

'Now's not the time to go all eco-warrior on us about pollution, Ella,' Saskia replied.

'I'm not. That crate is made of wooden pallets,' I said. 'Those pallets are light. We can use them to make a raft to get across the river!'

Grace frowned.

'Come on, help me pull it apart!' I said, excited.

The others shrugged and helped me drag the huge crate back from the water. We used our legs to kick it apart, leaving four flat pallets of wood.

'We can join these together to form one big raft,' I said. 'Let's pull them back to the dirt beach.'

We lugged the wooden pallets back to the cove and started to brainstorm how we could build a raft from them.

'Remember Martha said you need buoyant materials underneath the raft to make it float, and hollow things are good for buoyancy. I saw some bamboo plants on the way down. Bamboo is hollow—it must float! Grace, Saskia, go back up that trail and get a whole stack of it. Mercedes, open all of our packs and get the balls of twine out of the survival kits we were given,' I said.

My heart beat wildly with excitement. I couldn't

believe I'd had a survival idea and the others were following my lead!

Grace and Saskia gathered as much bamboo as they could, and we started to tie it together to form a base to go underneath the wooden pallet flooring of the raft. Saskia was careful to use only the amount of bamboo we needed to keep it afloat—she didn't want a repeat of her too-heavy raft from the day before.

'Mercedes, get the big pack of plastic bin bags from my pack and start bagging up our hiking packs. We don't want them getting wet,' I instructed.

'Great idea, Ella,' Grace said, smiling at me.

After a long while, we finally stood back to admire our handiwork. The raft was ready.

We pushed it into the shallows of the river, being careful to hold onto it so it didn't rush downstream.

'Does it float?' Mercedes yelled from the embankment.

'Yes!' I yelled back, gleeful.

'Hop on, Grace, and we'll see if it takes weight,' I said. 'Saskia and I will hold the raft steady.'

Grace climbed onto the raft. It creaked a little and bobbed about, but even with Grace kneeling on it, the bottom of the raft was barely submerged beneath the surface of the water.

'It's great!' I yelled.

'Do you think it will hold us all? And our packs?' Saskia asked nervously.

'It's our only shot,' I shrugged.

It had to work.

Chapter 10

We put the hiking packs, covered in garbage bags, in the centre of the raft to keep it steady. Then one by one, we climbed onboard. It bobbed around, as if irritated by our weight, but stayed afloat. We each held a long branch we'd stuck in the riverbed to hold us in place until we were ready. Then we could use them either as paddles or to push us away from rocks.

The river was flowing at an even pace—not too fast but also not slowly. Once we got into the middle, we were probably going to move at a speed similar to that of running along the bank.

'Maybe we can use the raft to follow the trail downstream,' I said. 'It would be quicker and might even catch us up to the others before nightfall.'

When Grace and Saskia nodded, I looked up and traced the arc of the sun towards the horizon. It wouldn't be too long until sundown— we had to make up some ground after stopping for so long at the riverbank.

'On the count of three, everyone pull your sticks up and use them to push us away from the rocks,' I said. 'One, two, THREE!'

We lifted our branches and used them to propel us away from the bank. I suddenly felt very nervous without the security of dry ground. The current of the river swept us up and pushed us smoothly but quickly down the river. Thankfully, the water was pretty flat and the ride was gentle.

'We did it!' Mercedes yelled.

'Ella did it!' Grace corrected, winking at me.

I felt a warmth flood through my chest. I *had* done it.

We glided along the river, watching the riverbank

zoom by beside us and keeping an eye on the trail. Every now and then we would need to use our branches to navigate us away from a rock, but it was easy work. I put my fingertips in the water, allowing it to rush over my hand as we floated along. It was cool and pleasant and I wriggled my fingers to stop them from numbing. While the air around us was still warm enough, I didn't want to fall in the river at this temperature. It would be freezing, and the last thing we needed was to be cold and wet and unable to dry ourselves properly.

'Ah, this is the life,' Mercedes said, lying back to soak in the sun.

'Who'd have thought the four of us would have ended up together?' Grace asked, laughing.

'No offence, but I wouldn't have *chosen* you two as my camping companions,' Saskia said with her eyebrow raised, looking at me and Grace.

I shook my head at Saskia. I'd known her the whole time I'd been at Eden College, and our relationship had been fractious from the beginning. *Fractious* is a big word that means getting into fights easily.

There was something about me and Saskia that just didn't mix well. Like oil and water. Nanna Kate says that girls like Saskia are often mean because they are jealous. Maybe that was true. All I knew was that I was never really sure where I stood with Saskia. She could be kind when she wanted to be, but she could also be really mean. Maybe this camp was just what we needed to get to know the better side of each other.

'Maybe Mrs Sinclair was right after all,' I mused. 'Maybe camp really *is* for finding out new things about other people.'

'And maybe you can actually function without your BFF, Zoe, always at your side,' Saskia quipped.

I frowned. Was it obvious to everyone that I relied on Zoe so much?

But look at me now! Floating on a raft that we had constructed from *my own* ideas. I'd show everyone that I could survive without my bestie. I'd show them all that—

'Are we moving faster?' Mercedes asked, sitting up from her sunbaking position.

I glanced around. The riverbank *did* seem to be flying past at a blistering pace.

The raft creaked.

BANG!

We all screamed as the water splashed up onto us.

'It was just a rock—we're OK,' Grace said, pushing her stick into the water to try and slow us down.

We were definitely picking up speed and were now hurtling down the river. Images from movies where people ended up going over waterfalls or smashing into rocks flashed into my mind. We weren't even wearing life jackets!

'Do you think we should head to the other side of the bank now? Start walking?' I asked nervously.

The others all nodded furiously.

'We just need to get over there, out of the current. Everyone, dig your sticks into the riverbed and try to push us in that direction,' Saskia said.

We tried, but the river seemed to have gotten stronger. When Saskia jabbed her branch into the riverbed, it snapped in half and floated away.

The raft creaked again. I swallowed hard. We really needed to get to the other side and off this raft before it fell apart and we lost our supplies.

'Paddle harder, Grace!' I yelled.

BANG!

We screamed as we hit another rock.

'Help!'

We turned abruptly to see Mercedes was in the water, rushing downstream behind us.

'Mercedes!' Saskia shrieked.

I crawled to the back of the raft and held out my stick so she could grab onto it. Mercedes reached out and seized the stick and I pulled her towards me. But the river was moving so fast, she couldn't haul herself back on the raft.

'Just keep holding onto the raft!' I yelled.

We continued to race down the river, our packs still in the centre of the raft and Mercedes hanging onto the back for dear life. The raft groaned and creaked, and one of the bamboo logs floated out from underneath the wooden pallet.

'We need to get to shore!' I yelled.

'Look!' Grace shrieked, pointing. Over towards the bank up ahead, there was what looked like a large rockpool. It was protected by a build-up of sticks and rocks, forming its own little shallow bay. And it was big enough to fit our raft. 'We need to get in there!'

Saskia moved to the back of the raft to hold onto Mercedes' wrists, just to make sure we didn't lose her when we turned. I took my branch paddle up to the front with Grace and tried to help her steer the raft towards the protected little bay.

'We only have one shot at this, or we are going to miss it!' Grace yelled. 'On the count of three, dig your branch in and push as hard as you can to drive us to the right!'

'One!'

'Please hurry!' Mercedes wailed.

'Two!'

'Come on, guys, you can do it!' Saskia shrieked.

'THREE!'

Grace and I dug our sticks into the riverbed and

pushed hard, and the raft was violently shunted to the right. Our hiking packs slid dangerously close to the edge, but Saskia used her legs to stop them from tumbling into the river. One of the straps on Saskia's pack snapped open though, and the tent, which had been attached, plunged into the water below.

'The tent!' Saskia screamed, trying to reach it with one hand while still holding onto Mercedes with the other.

'Leave it!' I yelled. 'It's too dangerous!'

The tent surged ahead of the raft and crashed into a pile of rocks, before spinning off down river.

'Not *another* tent!' Grace moaned. 'Now we've lost *two!'*

Remembering it was actually our tent that Saskia was carrying because we'd won the raft race on the lake, I winced.

Then I realised the raft was about to crash into the same pile of rocks as the tent. I jammed my stick into the riverbed again. The raft lurched as some of the bamboo pieces shot out from under us and were carried downstream, before we spun around 180 degrees and caught on the rocks forming the edge of the rock pool. With one final push, Grace and I drove the raft into the safety of the bay.

'You did it!' Saskia yelled.

The water flowing through the tiny bay was much gentler. We were able to hoist Mercedes back onto the raft, where she sat shivering violently. Then we used our branches to push the raft over to the riverbank, right next to the hiking trail.

Despite our best efforts, the raft crashed into the embankment with some force, sending our packs rolling onto the wet rocks of the shore. We quickly got off the raft and pulled them up to the dry grass. Behind us, the current picked up the raft and tugged it out of the safety of the little rock pool, sending it back into the flow of the fast moving river.

As we all lay gasping and breathless on the riverbank, the raft gave a final groan and cracked apart. We watched as multiple bamboo pieces rushed downstream, and the pallet smashed apart on some large boulders about 20 metres away.

I wiped the water out of my eyes and looked up in breathless relief. And for a split second, I saw a figure on the rocks on the opposite side of the river, looking across at us, her silver hair whipping around her face. I reached out to tap Grace to show her, but the minute I took my eyes off the figure, she disappeared.

Chapter 11

Dear Diary,

You wouldn't believe what an adventure this trip has turned into! Mercedes fell over the edge of a cliff, we got lost in the bush, and we managed to make a raft out of bamboo and crates and it actually worked! I've never been so proud. I'm totally going to add a survival section to my article for Eden Press, explaining how to make a raft when you're lost in the wild.

It's scary being left alone in the wilderness, but here's the creepiest thing, Diary. I keep spotting the

Mount Midnight witch! I wrote about her the other night when I couldn't stop thinking about Portia's story. And I've seen her! She has silvery hair that looks long and wild. And here's the scariest part—I think she's stalking us! I saw her at the lake and then at the lookout and then again at the river. She must be tracking us. But she's still really far away, so she hasn't caught up to us yet. Part of me is really scared she might find us, but after seeing how well we survived the river rafting, maybe we could take her on?!

We are all exhausted from our hike and river adventure and are sitting down to have some water and a rest. But Mercedes is still wet and I can see her teeth are chattering. I'm really worried about her. I'd better go and talk to the others about what we should do . . .

Love,

Ella

'Tinned spaghetti, bread and . . . custard powder—just add water!' Saskia said, holding up a sachet. 'What have you guys got?'

Grace pulled out a few apples, a tin of meatballs and some carrot sticks.

I held up a small bag of rice and some hot chocolate powder.

'Not too bad,' Saskia said, shrugging. 'There's definitely enough here for dinner tonight and breakfast tomorrow. We should catch up to the others before lunch. How are you going, Mercedes?'

Mercedes sat wrapped in a small chamois towel, her teeth chattering. The sun was still up and she was able to sit in the sunshine, drying her hiking boots, pants and socks. But as I saw the edges of the sky turn slightly orange, I knew we didn't have too much longer. Once the sun was down, she'd be freezing.

'We need to get a fire going, fast,' I said.

Grace and Saskia agreed, and we began gathering the different types of sticks we needed to build the fire.

Martha had told us to use grasses that burn easily to get the first flame going. But then we'd need to place some bigger sticks and then logs onto it so it would burn well into the night.

Grace formed a circle of rocks around the patch of dirt we planned to light the fire on, and we piled the kindling within easy reach.

'Does anyone have a lighter?' she asked. 'Or matches?'

We rummaged through our packs, and Saskia managed to find a small box of matches in her emergency kit. The only problem was they'd been kept in the front pocket of her hiking pack, which had gotten wet in the raft incident. They were useless.

'How else can we light a flame?' I asked desperately.

'Does anyone have glasses? Or a magnifying glass?' Saskia asked.

We all shook our heads.

'Let's try rubbing sticks together really fast, like in the movies,' Grace suggested.

I shrugged. It couldn't hurt to try.

But it *did* hurt to try. After what seemed like hours of rubbing the sticks together, our hands were aching and the most we'd gotten from them was a bit of heat. At no stage did we get a spark.

'This is hopeless!' Saskia yelled, throwing the sticks into the bush.

'It's OK, guys, I'm almost dry now,' Mercedes called from her spot in the sun. She'd pulled off her t-shirt and was lying on the warm rocks in her crop top, sunning her tummy.

'But it's going to get cold soon, Mercedes, and we need to cook our dinner,' Saskia complained.

Mercedes sat up slightly, leaning on her elbows so she could look at us. As she did, a bright glare flashed into my eyes.

'Ow, that's bright! What is that?' I asked, shielding my eyes.

'It's coming from your necklace,' Grace said, covering her eyes with her hand.

'Oh, this? It's my necklace from Italy. Venetian glass, you know. It's really cool—on this island, they have these guys who make beautiful glass ornaments and jewellery out of liquid glass. They use special tools to blow it into shape. I got this drop-crystal shape, even though I wanted the unicorn, but my mother said the unicorn was too gaudy, whatever that means,' Mercedes nattered.

'It means flashy and over the top,' I said quickly, waving my hand dismissively. 'And we know, you told us on the bus . . . wait—'

'Well, thank you very much, Miss Dictionary, but I'll have you know this is *not* over the top—'

She stopped as I rushed over and grabbed the pendant hanging from her neck in the palm of my hand.

'Very chic, right?' she said, smiling.

'More like lifesaving,' I murmured. 'Can I borrow this for a second?'

Mercedes frowned.

'Look how it magnifies the sunlight. We can light a fire with this, Mercedes!' I said.

'Oh, right,' she said, slipping the leather necklace over her head and handing it to me.

‘Who knew Mercedes’ expensive fashion taste would save the day?’ Grace laughed. ‘Do you think it will work?’

‘Not for much longer—the sun is getting low. Let’s do this,’ I said, taking the necklace over to our campfire circle and handing it to Grace.

Saskia crushed up some bark, just like we had been shown to do when lighting a fire in our survival lesson. Then I added some of the very dry husks of dead grass that we knew would burn easily. Grace looked up at the angle of the sun and held the pendant over the tinder. She moved the pendant around until the sunlight was shining directly through the ridges of the charm, making the light concentrate into a tiny point, then kept it very still.

We all held our breath.

The tinder blackened under the focal point of the light beam and began to smoke. We all squealed in excitement, and the smoke stopped immediately as Grace’s hand moved.

‘Whoops,’ I whispered. ‘Try again.’

Grace held the pendant still again, and as the smoke began to rise from the dry pile of grass, she gently blew on it.

'Why is she blowing it out?' Mercedes whispered.

'She's not. She's giving it more oxygen, which fire needs to burn,' Saskia explained.

Suddenly, a tiny orange flicker danced to life. The grass tinder went up in flames instantly, but it quickly started to die down, just as we expected it would. Now we had to try to keep the fire alive by getting the bigger sticks to catch.

Grace carefully added small sticks and twigs in a pyramid formation over the flame. The sticks began to burn and we hopped up and down with anticipation. Slowly, we added more, and as the bigger sticks began to catch, we pulled over the larger pieces of wood, which would likely burn for many hours if we could get them to light.

A couple of times we almost snuffed out the fire with the weight of the heavier wood, but we learned to be careful and gentle as we gradually built the fire up.

Finally, it burned independently, crackling with life, just like it did last night when we were at the campsite with the rest of our year level.

'You did it!' I said, giving Grace a hug.

'Not without your and Mercedes' help,' she smiled, handing back the pendant.

'And just in time too. It'll be sunset soon,' Saskia said. 'Look!'

We moved away from our little campsite clearing, back towards the river, to watch the sun returning to its home for the night. The golden orb seemed to sizzle on the horizon as the sky lit up pink and orange. It reminded me of one of Max's finger paintings from when he was younger. Nanna Kate always said that somewhere out there, someone was doing a majestic sky-painting each night, and it certainly looked true tonight, with streaks and swirls and burning colours dipping into the cool of the water below.

It was utterly sublime. That's a fancy word for beautiful and breathtaking. I only use it to describe really special things, like a gorgeous sunset or a stunning painting or my mum in her favourite formal dress.

Grace leaned her head on my shoulder as we took in nature's spectacle. It made me think back to camping trips with my family, and I felt my emotions catch in my throat. What I wouldn't give to be sitting with Mum right at this moment, her arms wrapped around me, watching the sunset together. Or to be with Dad, making hot chocolate by the campfire. Or even to be with Max and Olivia, collecting bugs in the bush. I sighed at the memory and gently linked my arm through Grace's. She wasn't family, but this was as close as I would get to being with the people I loved the most.

Chapter 12

Once the sun had returned to its den, we headed back to our makeshift campsite. The fire was still crackling away, as the flames greedily licked the thicker pieces of wood we had put onto it. We used our torches as little lanterns, lighting the area around us. Then we treated, boiled and cooled water from the river to create more drinking water, and started to pull out our camping saucepans to heat up the food for dinner. While Saskia and I cooked, Mercedes and Grace cleared a space to set up the tent.

'Looks like we'll be sleeping under the stars tonight,'

Grace said suddenly, crouched next to our four packs. I looked over and realised none of us were carrying a tent. Grace and I had given our tent to Saskia to carry, and it was somewhere at the bottom of Mount Midnight River now. And there was no tent attached to Mercedes' backpack either.

'Mercedes, what happened to your tent?' I asked.

She shrugged. 'It was too heavy, so I gave it to one of the rangers this morning.'

We all groaned.

'We are going to get eaten by mosquitos,' Grace wailed, scratching already.

'Don't forget the bug repellent then,' Saskia said, tossing the spray over to Grace.

I put some on too, remembering that I was a complete mozzie-magnet.

After we ate our dinner, Grace dug out a stash of marshmallows from the bottom of her pack. We each chose sticks and used them to gently char the treats over the fire, pulling off the marshmallow skin and licking the melted centre.

'Maybe this isn't so bad after all,' Mercedes said, popping a whole marshmallow into her mouth.

'Anyone got any campfire stories?' Grace asked.

I shook my head violently. 'No more ghost stories,' I said. 'Portia's story has been stuck in my head for a whole day now. Did you know I keep seeing an old lady, standing on the cliffs looking at us? Do you think it's that Esmerelda Midnight witch?'

Saskia, Mercedes and Grace laughed. 'It's probably just your big imagination, Ella,' Saskia said.

I wasn't convinced.

The stars began to appear in the sky, like holes poked into a black canopy above, revealing the dazzling light behind. We removed our boots and shimmied into our sleeping bags fully clothed, nestling up closely together. The air had turned cold and we would need to keep each other warm throughout the night. Luckily, all our sleeping bags were made for very cold conditions, so I was confident we'd be OK in them.

'Sleeping under the stars is actually pretty cool,' Grace said, gazing up at the sky.

'As long as it doesn't rain,' Saskia laughed.

We lay there in silence, listening to the sounds of the bush. As the daytime species quietened to sleep, the creatures of the night began to wake and sing to each other in the crisp night air.

Then I heard a howl in the distance.

'What was that?' I said, sitting up with a start.

'Just animals,' Grace said. But I thought I detected a tiny quiver in her voice.

'Sounded like a wolf,' I whispered, lying down again.

'We should be OK with the campfire,' Saskia said, trying to sound confident.

I nodded in the dark, more for myself than for the others. But images kept flashing into my mind of Esmerelda's lost wolf-dog. We lay there in silence for some time, and I thought everyone had drifted off to sleep. Then Saskia rolled over.

'Ella?' Saskia whispered through the darkness.

'Yeah?'

'You were really brave today,' she said quietly. Her voice seemed softer in the night air. 'Making that raft and helping Grace drive us to safety on the water—that was . . . really cool.'

'Thanks, Saskia,' I whispered.

Then I snuggled into my sleeping bag and let the sounds of the night carry me off to sleep.

I dreamed of hiking up a big steep hill. There were echidnas among the trees, looking at me with their spines raised on their backs. Every time I took a step forward, I slipped back down two steps. I looked all around me, but knew I was alone, though I could see curious eyes peeking at me through the dense bush. I trudged on, trying to get to the top of the hill, which now felt more like a mountain. I squinted and saw a house at the top of the mountain. It was my house. My house from home, not Eden College. I could see through the windows, which were lit with a gentle glow. Inside were my mum and dad, my sister, Olivia, and my brother, Max. They were all sitting down to Christmas lunch. Zoe and Nanna Kate were also at the table.

I yelled out to them, but they couldn't hear me.

I ran up the hill, but it felt like I was running on the spot. I pushed myself harder and harder, desperate to get to the top. But when I finally got there, my house looked completely different. I nervously crept to the door and saw it was ajar. I pushed it gently and it swung open with a creak. Suddenly, the hallway inside lit up, and there, standing in front of me, was a tall woman with a witch's hat over her long silver hair. She cackled when she saw me and reached out with her long bony fingers. In the background, a wolf let out a long, terrifying howl.

I woke up with a scream and sat bolt upright. My forehead was damp with sweat and I was breathing as fast as I would have been if I'd just run a race.

'Are you OK, Ella?' a croaky voice mumbled from next to me.

'I'm OK, Grace. Just a bad dream.' I tried to slow my breathing down.

'Come here,' Grace said, patting the ground close to her body. I snuggled in next to her.

'You're cold,' she mumbled.

She could obviously feel me shivering. But I wasn't cold at all. I shut my eyes tightly and started to hum one of my favourite songs, trying to drown out the echoes of the wolf's howl from my dream.

Chapter 13

The sun rose early and I woke as it shone down into my face. The morning birds were up and singing and the light rush of the river instantly reminded me where we were.

I sat up, rubbing my eyes. Mercedes, Grace and Saskia were all curled in on either side of me, like a little pack of wolf cubs sleeping in a den. We had kept each other warm overnight, and the gentle sound of the river flowing had been a soothing soundtrack to lull us all to sleep, even after my nightmare. One by one the others stirred, all bleary eyes and matted hair.

Saskia walked down to the river and washed her face to help wake herself up.

We calculated that the rest of our year group would probably be reaching the end point just before lunchtime. So we would need to hurry if we were going to catch up to them.

But what was going to happen when we got there? Could we just sneak in and join them without being noticed? How were we ever going to explain this to Coach Bright? I shook the thought out of my head. The priority right now was getting everyone there safely. I'd worry about the consequences of what we'd done later.

After a simple breakfast of campfire toast and tinned spaghetti, we washed out our pots and plates and packed everything up into our hiking packs. We filled our drink bottles with purified water, making sure we had enough for the next few hours of hiking. I smeared sunscreen over my arms and face and pulled a fresh pair of light hiking pants over my legs. Then Grace braided my hair, before I slipped my school cap onto my head and pulled my long braid through the hole in the back.

Once our packs were securely fastened and settled on our shoulders, we headed down the trail snaking its way alongside the river. It was a flat, easy walk, and I was glad we'd made the decision to follow the river trail instead of trying to hike around the mountain.

'Look, a sign!' Grace said, racing over to a wooden board with a plaque attached to it.

The sign showed that we were only eight kilometres away from the second base camp. And it also showed that the trail we were on would lead us there. I wondered if we'd see any other people on the trail as we hiked. It was comforting to know that we were on the safety of a proper trail, and not trying to navigate our way through the bush on our own. Even so, we still used Mercedes' sparkly lipstick to mark a tree every now and then, pointing the arrow in the direction we were headed.

The trail was wide enough to walk two people side-by-side. Saskia and Mercedes walked in front of me and Grace. From the back they almost looked like twins, with their matching long braids hanging down their backs, one black, one blonde.

'Do you think we're going to get into a mountain of trouble when we get there?' I asked Grace in a wavering voice.

'Probably,' she shrugged. 'But I think the priority right now is to get there safe and sound. We'll deal with Monty then.'

I nodded.

'Besides, we've had the best adventure, don't you think?' she added, her green eyes shining with the excitement of our survival alone in the wild.

'Yeah, we have,' I said, smiling back. 'And who'd have thought I could have done it without Zoe by my side?' I laughed.

Grace frowned. 'Why would you need Zoe?'

'It's like Saskia said—everyone thinks I'm always by her side. And she's not entirely wrong. I think I *do* use Zoe as a safety blanket,' I said, scrunching up my nose. 'I mean, we've been best friends since we were four. I can't think of any challenge I've had to face without her.

Even coming to Eden College! She's always been there for me.'

'And *you've* been there for *her*,' Grace added. 'You aren't the only one who benefits from your friendship, you know. Zoe needs you just as much as you need her.'

I frowned. I'd never thought about it that way. For some reason, I'd always seen Zoe as the anchor, with me holding onto her. But maybe I was just as much a security blanket for her as she was for me.

'And look at you out here,' Grace added. 'It was *your* idea to make the raft. And *you* spotted the necklace that started our fire. We'd have been stuck on the other side of the river if it wasn't for you, cold and hungry.'

I breathed in sharply. Grace was right! I felt a warm glow of pride and accomplishment rush through my body. 'Thanks, Grace,' I smiled.

Then we almost bumped into Mercedes and Saskia, who were standing still as statues in front of us.

'Hey, watch out!' Grace said, as she pulled up suddenly behind them.

'Sssh!' Mercedes hissed, remaining frozen.

A dark feeling of dread washed over me. I very slowly and carefully leaned to the right of Mercedes to see what they were looking at. And there in front of us, lying across the trail, was a long black snake. It was lying completely still, gazing into the bush, frozen.

'What do we do?' Saskia hissed through her clenched teeth.

'Stay calm,' Mercedes said, still not moving a muscle.

The snake suddenly twitched its tail, and I noticed the row of red markings where its underside touched the ground.

'It's a red-bellied black snake,' Mercedes whispered. 'They are venomous. We need to be still.'

Fear gripped my throat. I felt dizzy and my mouth went dry. The snake lay still again, staring, its forked tongue flicking in and out of its mouth.

'Should I get a stick and try to scare it away?' Saskia whispered.

'No. Stay still. Remember what Martha said when we saw the echidna?' Mercedes said quietly. 'Most wildlife is more scared of us than we are of it.'

'I don't know about that . . . I'm pretty scared,' I mumbled.

'Just stay still,' Mercedes warned.

'Let's run back,' Saskia whimpered.

'Stay STILL,' Mercedes ordered.

The snake began to move.

Saskia let out a squeak and shuffled her foot, ready to run.

'STAY STILL!' Mercedes hissed again.

The snake glanced in our direction, but then turned its body and began gliding up the trail in front of us. Its body looked like liquid as it moved effortlessly across the earth. It was much faster than I expected it to be, and I was suddenly glad we hadn't run—it would have caught up to us easily in a chase. It slithered silently on, leaving a smooth, curved print in the dirt behind it. My muscles started to relax as I noticed the beauty of the creature in front of us. The snake turned and slipped into the scrub off the side of the trail.

We exhaled as one and all sat down in the dirt, our hearts thumping.

'Good job, Mercedes,' I said, shaking my head.

'What did I do?' she asked.

'You were right to make us keep still. If that was me by myself, I would have run,' I said.

Mercedes tried to hide her obvious pride.

'Do you think it's gone now?' Grace asked.

'I think so,' Mercedes said. 'To be safe, we can walk very slowly and loudly on the other side of the trail to make sure it hears us coming and we are as far away from it as possible. We don't want to surprise it or make it feel threatened if it's still there.'

We all nodded and stood up. Then we stomped up the trail, past the place where it had disappeared into the scrub. Once we were several metres further on, we all began to relax.

Being left behind. Cliff rescues. Raging rivers. Making our own fire. Facing a venomous snake. Surely there couldn't be any *more* drama on this trip, could there?

Chapter 14

Dear Diary,

You'll never believe it, but Mercedes just saved us from a venomous snake. Mercedes! She knew exactly what type of snake it was and how we should react. I never knew Mercedes was such an expert on wildlife. I wonder if there are other things I don't know about her? For my Eden Press article, I think I'm going to get Mercedes to come and do a guest-report section about identifying dangerous snakes in the bush. She seems to know a lot about them. We are so close to the end point, I can almost feel it.

Even though I have no idea what kind of trouble we'll be in when we arrive, I can't help but be excited. We've survived a night alone in the bush and trekking through Mount Midnight all on our own! All we have to do is follow the river and we'll be back with our class. I can't wait to see them all. Even Monty! Better go—we've almost finished our rest.

Love,

Ella

I took the last bite of my apple and closed my notebook, then slipped it and my pen into my backpack and zipped the bag up. I took a long drink from my water bottle, gazing up at the sky. We'd been so lucky with the clear skies and sunshine so far, but I noticed a few grey clouds dotted on the horizon. They had a green tinge to them and looked a little foreboding. A storm would definitely be bad. We were so close to the end and I didn't want anything getting in the way of us making it back to our group before the alarm was raised that we were missing. I pulled out my roll-on sunscreen and glided the ball along my arms and legs, rubbing the cream in. While it wasn't a blazing hot day, I was still being careful to not get burnt. I slipped my school PE cap back onto my head.

'Are we ready?' I said cheerfully to the others, who were still taking long gulps from their water bottles.

I picked up my pack and flung it over my shoulders, then secured the straps and buckles, allowing the weight to redistribute across my torso. I felt so much more at ease while carrying my pack now, especially compared to the first time I'd picked it up. Maybe this outdoorsy thing did suit me after all!

Mercedes used her lipstick to mark a tree to show the direction we were heading. Grace picked up the scraps of wrappers from our muesli bars and put them into her pack. Then the four of us set off along the track again, keeping an eye out for snakes or any other wildlife that might have wandered onto the trail.

As we walked on, the light slowly started to dissipate. It was still early in the day, but those threatening grey clouds on the horizon seemed to be blowing over to us much quicker than I'd expected.

Grace sniffed the air like a wolf. 'I think I can smell rain coming,' she said.

'Petrichor,' I said, matter-of-factly.

'What?' Mercedes asked.

'Petrichor. It's the name given to the smell when it's about to rain,' I said.

'Petrichor,' Mercedes repeated. 'How do you know so many big words, Ella?'

I shrugged. 'I think it's because I read a lot.'

'Is that why you're such a brainiac?' Mercedes teased.

'Better than being an airhead,' Saskia laughed.

Mercedes stopped. 'That's not funny, Saskia,' she said flatly.

'Oh, I'm only joking, Mercedes,' Saskia sang.

'But it's not funny,' Mercedes persisted.

'Well, you've got to admit, sometimes you do say some pretty silly things, Mercedes,' Saskia said, sounding irritated.

Grace and I exchanged glances.

'Come on, don't fight now,' Grace mumbled.

'I'm not fighting,' Mercedes said. 'I just get a little tired of everyone always thinking I'm not smart.'

Saskia rolled her eyes. Mercedes moved to walk alongside Grace, and Saskia smothered the look of hurt in her eyes by shaking her head and shrugging, as if she didn't care.

A low rumble of thunder sounded in the distance.

'Let's play Would You Rather,' Grace said, trying to change the mood. 'Would you rather have teeth for hair or hair for teeth?'

'What?'

'Gross!'

'Teeth for *hair*?'

'I'd go hair for teeth,' Grace said. 'At least I could shut my mouth and you wouldn't see it.'

'But imagine all the hair that would get caught in your food!' I laughed.

'This is gross,' Saskia said, refusing to participate in the game.

I suddenly stopped. Ahead, the path forked into two, with one trail leading up into the bush and the other following the river. I looked from side to side, then began to walk up the path that followed the river.

'Why are you going that way?' Saskia asked.

'We're following the river. That's the plan,' I said.

'Yeah, but the river curves this way and that for ages. Didn't you see from the lookout? I think this other trail will take us directly to the base camp,' Saskia said, pointing at the trail on the left of the fork, which disappeared into the bush.

'But what if it doesn't?' Grace said. 'I think the river is the safest bet.'

'It's obviously still a trail. It can't lead to nowhere,' Saskia said, her voice rising in irritation.

'The last thing we need to do now is get lost,' I said, folding my arms across my chest.

'The last thing we need to do now is waste time winding along the river and risk missing out on meeting up with the rest of our grade because we're too slow,' Saskia said in a loud voice. 'Mercedes?'

Mercedes looked from her friend to me and Grace. She looked at the paths in front and then down at her feet. Then she frowned and looked up. 'I think Ella's right,' she said flatly.

Saskia's cheeks burned red. 'Thanks a lot, Mercedes!' she shouted.

'You asked my opinion,' Mercedes yelled back.

'Please, stop fighting,' Grace breathed, sounding like a frustrated parent.

'This is because I *joked* that you're an airhead, isn't it?' Saskia accused, pointing her finger at Mercedes.

'No, this is because your idea is dumb!' Mercedes yelled back.

'Oh, that's rich.'

'Why don't you stop and think about why we are even here, Saskia!' Mercedes yelled back. 'This is because of *your* dumb idea. It was *you* who wanted to change which groups we were in. It was *you* who rubbed our names off the lists and didn't put them back on. Nobody even knows we are lost and it is all *your* fault!'

Saskia's face burned with anger. Her eyes were narrow and her skin was flushed pink. She looked at each one of us. 'Fine! I'll go the *quick* way, and I'll get to the camp way before you.'

She began to march up the other path.

'We can't split up!' I yelled after Saskia. 'If something happens to you, you'll be on your own!'

'Saskia, come back,' Grace pleaded.

But Saskia put her head down and stomped up the trail into the bush. I went to follow her, but Mercedes held my arm. 'She's just being dramatic,' she said.

'We're not leaving!' Grace yelled after her. 'We are staying right here until you turn around and come back!'

Saskia ignored us.

'She'll come back,' Mercedes laughed bitterly. 'She's just annoyed we aren't following her stupid plan. We'll wait five minutes and she'll be back.'

Grace and I looked at each other. I could see the worry in Grace's eyes and I was sure she could see the worry in mine. We put our packs on the ground and sat down on top of them. Then we all took a sip of water from our bottles.

'Saskia! Come baaaack!' Grace yelled every couple of minutes.

The sun disappeared as the grey clouds rolled in. The rumble of thunder became more frequent. Slowly, fat drops of rain began to fall into the dirt, splashing my boots.

We waited five minutes.

Then ten.

'Are you sure she's coming back?' I asked Mercedes in a wavering voice.

'She usually does,' Mercedes whispered. But the quiver in her voice betrayed her.

We waited and waited.

But Saskia didn't return.

Chapter 15

The chubby drops of rain turned into bullets of water, pelting down on us. We pulled out our splash jackets, but they did nothing against the deluge of water that was coming from the sky. The dusty trail beneath us almost instantly turned into a slippery mud bath, caking sludge onto our boots and splashing it up over our ankles.

'We need to find her,' Mercedes yelled over the torrent of rain.

Grace and I looked at each other and nodded.

'She's got a decent head start on us, though.

We're going to have to move fast,' Grace replied.

We pulled our packs on over our splash jackets and began speed-walking along the trail that Saskia had disappeared up earlier. It had more of an incline than the flat path beside the river, and we found ourselves slipping backward every few steps as the track turned into a mudslide. I slipped onto my hands and knees twice, but Grace and Mercedes helped me up each time.

The thunder continued to rumble and the rain became heavier.

As we moved along, we noticed the trail was becoming less defined. It was narrower too—it felt like the bush was closing in on us. It meant we were more protected from the rain, but it also meant everything around us seemed even darker than before.

'Saskia!' Grace hollered.

'Wait, what's that?' Mercedes said, jogging further up the trail and bending over. She turned around, holding Saskia's cap.

'It probably just fell off her pack,' I said.

Mercedes nodded, but looked concerned. She looped Saskia's cap onto a strap on her bag and urged us to keep going at a quicker pace. I could tell she was feeling bad about the fight she'd just had with her friend, and she was worried. It reminded me of the time I lost Max at the shops. He was only about five years old and we were meant to wait in the food court while Mum took Olivia to the toilets. Max kept trying to convince me to take him into the toy shop. When I said no, he tried to sneak off to go in by himself. I thought I'd teach him a lesson and I hid so that he'd be worried when he came back and saw I was gone. But then he didn't come back. By the time Mum found me again, I was crying because *I'd* lost *him*. Turns out she'd seen him looking at the toys on the way back from the toilets, and she'd had him with her all along. But for those moments where I thought I'd lost him, I felt like the worst big sister in the whole wide world.

'We'll find her,' I said to Mercedes, gently patting her arm.

She frowned. 'Let's go faster,' she said resolutely.

We walked on, slipping and sliding, calling out to Saskia every so often. But then Mercedes, who was still walking at the front, stopped dead in her tracks. She turned back to me and Grace, and her face was pale. Her eyes were wide and her lips quivered. We rushed up beside her as she pointed along the track.

There, lying on the ground, was Saskia's hiking pack.

But Saskia was nowhere to be seen.

Chapter 16

Panic washed over me like a monster wave at the beach. Grace and I screamed Saskia's name, looking around in wild alarm. What if a dingo had taken her? What if she'd fallen and broken her leg?

But Mercedes looked at the ground around the discarded hiking pack. 'Look!' she said. 'Footprints!'

We gathered close and looked at the footprints around the pack. They were indented into the now muddy track, which was sloppy with the rain. One set matched the size shoe we expected Saskia to have. But there was another set of prints. My neck prickled like someone was watching me.

'They look like adult feet,' Mercedes said.

The footprints seemed to dance around in a circle and then trailed off ahead. The adult prints walked in a straight line, but Saskia's prints appeared smudged and unsteady.

'Maybe she's found help!' Grace said hopefully.

'Let's follow them!' Mercedes yelled.

We ran as fast as we could with our hiking packs, Grace and I lugging Saskia's pack between us, up the trail to see where the footprints led. Ahead, we saw a small curl of smoke twisting above the top of the trees. As we broke through the more dense shrubbery, we came to a small cottage.

'The footprints lead to the house!' Mercedes said. 'Come on!'

'But what if it's dangerous?' I asked in a shaky voice.

'We have to be brave,' Mercedes insisted fiercely. 'For Saskia!'

So we ran up to the cottage, keeping low. We crept to the side wall, dropped Saskia's pack and tried to look in through the clouded, dirty windows. It was hard to see inside as raindrops streaked the glass, but it looked like a simple living room. There was a wooden table with only one chair. Adjoining the living area was a small kitchen with a kettle, a toaster and a microwave. A log fire was burning in the corner. By the fire was a couch and two armchairs, facing towards the opposite window. There was an arm resting motionlessly on the side of one of the armchairs. Was it Saskia's arm?

We peered from side to side. There didn't seem to be anyone else in there. So we tapped lightly on the window.

'Saskia?' I hissed through the glass. 'Saskia!'

'Should we go knock on the door?' Grace asked.

My mind started to spin, and I suddenly thought about Esmerelda Midnight. Fear gripped my chest. I shook my head violently.

'We don't know who lives here, or if they are friendly,' I said. 'Let's not give ourselves away in case we need to rescue Saskia.'

So we kept lightly tapping the window, trying to get

the attention of Saskia, who was hopefully the person in the armchair. But with the rain thumping down, it was obvious that whoever was in there couldn't hear us.

Suddenly, a voice crackled behind us. 'What have we here?'

We all screamed, startled to learn someone was standing right behind us. We spun around and standing in front of us was a tall woman we didn't know. She had weathered olive skin and deep brown eyes. She was frowning at us with her lips pursed. She wore khaki trousers and a khaki shirt, much like Martha had been wearing yesterday. But her hair was long and wavy and white with silver strands.

My mind raced. Was this the woman I'd seen on the clifftops?

Could this be Portia's witch . . . Esmerelda Midnight?

From inside the house, I suddenly heard a loud bark. I felt my head become light and I swayed on my feet.

It was just like my nightmare.

The path up the steep, slippery hill. Eyes watching me. The house at the top. Peeking in through the window.

People inside who couldn't hear me.

A tall woman with witch's hair and a howling dog.

I felt my head tip backwards.

Then everything went black.

'Just lie her down here. Has she been unwell?'

'No, I think she just got a fright.'

'Has she been drinking water?'

'Yes, here's her water bottle nearly empty.'

'What's her name?'

'Ella.'

'Ella? Ella?'

I opened my eyes slowly and found myself lying on a couch inside the cottage. Grace was holding my hand and Mercedes was sitting down by my feet. Across from me, Saskia sat in an armchair with a steaming mug of something warm. She had a thick bandage around her leg, but she was smiling.

And standing above me was the older woman from outside.

'Ella, are you feeling OK?' she asked in a warm voice.

I nodded, still feeling confused.

'I'm so sorry if I startled you. Do you want some hot chocolate like your friend Saskia has?' she asked.

'It's very good,' Saskia added.

I sat up slightly and nodded.

'I'm Elizabeth,' the older lady said. 'I'm one of the rangers here. Look,' she held out a card in front of her. It was an ID badge like the one all the other rangers were wearing. It showed a picture of her, looking slightly younger with strands of brown in her hair. The name 'Elizabeth Daley' was neatly printed underneath her picture. 'I've worked in the Mount Midnight National Park for over 40 years.'

'I'm sorry I fainted,' I said sheepishly. 'I got a fright. I thought you were . . .' I trailed off, too embarrassed to continue.

'The witch of Mount Midnight?' she laughed. 'I've heard that story before—about the old witch wandering the bushland looking for her dog?'

I nodded, blushing.

Elizabeth let out a loud warm chuckle. 'Well, I may not be a witch, but I do wander the bushland a lot and I do have a dog, so I'm not surprised. I lead groups of children on hikes all the time. I was actually meant to be one of the guides for the Eden College girls, but my dog was ill, so I chose not to lead this time. I didn't want to leave him.' Elizabeth nodded to the corner of the cottage. I hadn't noticed the big border collie lazing in the corner. 'He's all better now, though.'

Mercedes immediately jumped up and wandered over to the dog.

'Can I pat him?' she asked.

'Sure. He'll probably ignore you, but don't take offence—he's just old,' Elizabeth said.

Mercedes ducked down and extended her hand to the dog. He looked up and sniffed her steady outstretched hand.

'Heya, cutie,' she cooed.

The dog eyed her quizzically.

'His name is Wolf,' Elizabeth said.

Grace and I muffled a giggle.

'Hey, Wolfy-boy,' Mercedes said, as she gently massaged his head. Wolf appeared to be enjoying it, because he leant into her hand. When she paused, he nudged her to keep going.

'I guess I was wrong,' Elizabeth laughed. 'Wolf likes you!' She wandered into the kitchen section of the room and opened a pot that was sitting on the small stove. She ladled out three more mugs of hot chocolate for me, Mercedes and Grace, then walked back over and handed them to us. We took the warm drinks with thanks, still feeling chilled from the rain.

'I was just coming out to look for you three when I found you looking in my window,' she said.

'Saskia, why on earth did you leave your pack on the trail? We thought something terrible had happened,' Mercedes said.

Saskia smiled. 'Sorry about that! I hurt my leg,' she said, pointing down at the bandage wrapped around her calf. 'At first I thought a snake had bitten me, what with having seen that black snake on the path earlier and then suddenly feeling a sharp pain in my leg. So I screamed really loudly.'

'Loud enough to wake a wombat,' Elizabeth laughed. 'I came rushing down from my place, and the minute Saskia said it was a possible snake bite, I jumped straight into emergency mode. I lay her down to slow the venom while I located the bite to begin wrapping it. But when I saw the wound I immediately knew it was a scratch, not a snake bite. She'd obviously stepped on a sharp stick, which had created a long scratch down her leg. I've seen some snake bites in my time, I trained as a nurse originally, and they don't look at all like that, so that was an instant relief. I helped her back up to the cottage to get her out of the rain, but I didn't quite have the strength to carry her pack too.'

I raised my eyebrows, impressed that a woman of Elizabeth's age could carry Saskia, let alone a pack as well.

'I've patched Saskia up and she's just fine,' Elizabeth finished.

'Sure am!' Saskia beamed.

'Saskia told me how you four split up and so I was

coming back to find the rest of you. But you beat me to it, and found me first!' Elizabeth said. She sat down in the other armchair by the fire.

'Was it you I saw watching us from the clifftops?' I asked, sipping my hot chocolate. The smooth drink slipped down my throat and made my whole body feel warm and tingly.

'Yes, that was me,' Elizabeth said. 'I keep an eye on what's going on around the park, and I knew there was a group of Eden College girls here on camp. But it struck me as odd that there were four girls hiking alone. Sometimes we get teenagers hiking and camping as part of different programs, but they are usually much older if they are hiking without an adult. You girls looked very young to be alone. So I decided to hike down and find you. But when I got to the river, you'd disappeared. I figured you'd be somewhere along this trail, so that's when I started tracking you. I'm sorry I didn't find you before it got dark.'

'We were . . . separated from the group,' I said, embarrassed by our decision to trick the rangers.

'Saskia told me all about that too. It was a very naughty and dangerous thing you girls did,' Elizabeth said sternly.

Grace, Mercedes and I looked down guiltily.

'But it's something I probably would have done too, at your age,' Elizabeth went on with a wink.

'What do we do now?' I asked, looking at my watch. The rest of our grade would probably already be at the base camp by now.

'It's OK,' Elizabeth said. 'I've already called the rangers and explained that you are safe in my care. They've alerted your teachers that you were separated from the group, but reassured them that you are now in the care of a national park ranger and are safe.'

'So are we in a massive amount of trouble?' Grace asked.

Elizabeth paused. 'Probably.'

Our shoulders sank as the consequences of our actions started to bear down on us.

'But can I also say, you girls have done an incredible job of surviving in the bush by yourselves for a whole day and night. I was very impressed by what Saskia has been telling me. And I saw the lipstick markings on the trees—that made me realise that perhaps you girls were lost, not just hiking alone!'

We smiled at Mercedes, and Mercedes blushed. 'It's lipstick from Paris,' she said.

Elizabeth nodded. 'Of course. And goodness me, crossing the river on a raft you made yourselves? What ingenuity!' she gushed.

It was my turn to blush again now, pleased.

Grace looked out the window. 'Looks like it's still raining pretty heavily,' she said.

Elizabeth nodded. 'According to the radar, this storm is going to be short and sharp. It should clear as quickly as it arrived, and then we can get moving to the base camp to meet your friends.'

'We?' I asked.

'But of course. I'll lead you there. I even know a short cut,' Elizabeth winked. 'Go stand by the fire and dry yourselves off while you finish your hot chocolates. We can start making our way over once the rain eases up.'

I took another sip of the hot chocolate, feeling strengthened by the warm, sweet taste. The rain already sounded like it had started to ease. I stood up and wandered over to the crackling fire, standing with my back to it to allow the heat to seep into my wet t-shirt and pants. I looked out the window and then back to Elizabeth, shaking my head in silent disbelief. Who knew we'd end up having hot chocolates with the witch of Mount Midnight?

'Hey, Mercedes,' Elizabeth said, tilting her head to the side as she stared at Mercedes, who was still quietly murmuring to Wolf. 'You like animals, don't you?'

Mercedes nodded. 'I want to be a vet nurse.'

'Want to see something cool?' Elizabeth asked. 'Come over here . . .'

Chapter 17

Grace, Mercedes and I followed Elizabeth into a tiny little laundry room which adjoined the main living area. Saskia limped after us on her bandaged leg and leaned in through the doorway.

Elizabeth walked over to what looked like a mound of towels waiting to be washed, and scooped up a small blanket sewn into a pouch shape. She gently carried it in her arms, as careful as if she was carrying a newborn baby. She quietly opened the top of the pouch and we all leaned in for a closer look.

'Oh!' Mercedes gasped. 'It's a joey!'

A tiny baby joey lazily opened its eyes to look at us.

'This is Rosie,' Elizabeth said. 'Her mother was hit on the road. Thankfully, the drivers checked the pouch, because little Rosie here was inside. She was tiny with no hair and had no chance of surviving alone. I often rescue injured animals in the national park area. I've had Rosie a few weeks now and have been handfeeding her. Mercedes, would you like to hold the pouch?'

Mercedes' eyes lit up. 'Absolutely!' she said excitedly.

'I once helped look after a baby possum with a lady who rescues animals near my home,' I told Elizabeth proudly.

'How wonderful that you girls are all so caring for wildlife,' Elizabeth smiled. 'Would you like to feed her?'

Mercedes looked as if she was going to burst with happiness. Elizabeth led her back to one of the armchairs in the lounge and passed her a bottle of what looked like milk. Rosie immediately knew what was coming, and began sniffing the air with anticipation.

Mercedes guided the bottle into Rosie's mouth and she began to drink heartily.

'Wow, she sure does tug when she sucks on the bottle!' Mercedes said, amazed. 'She's about six months old, right?'

'That's right, Mercedes,' Elizabeth said, impressed. 'You know a lot about Australian wildlife!'

'But she thought drop bears were real up until a few days ago,' Saskia whispered under her breath. Grace frowned at her and Saskia rolled her eyes and walked back over to her own armchair.

I watched Mercedes as she fed Rosie. Rosie was tucked right into her chest like a tiny baby. Mercedes very quietly hummed as she fed her, and the joey seemed very calm and happy. Mercedes' eyes sparkled with joy and a passion I'd never really seen in her before. She looked completely content.

Slowly, the sound of the rain began to ease. Mercedes finished feeding Rosie, and Elizabeth helped put her back into her blanket nest in the laundry.

'Right, girls,' Elizabeth said, clapping her hands.

'Time to hit the road!'

'My leg still hurts quite a bit,' Saskia complained. 'This is going to take forever!'

'Not the way I see it. I've got a plan,' Elizabeth said, winking. Then she waved for us all to follow her outside.

We traipsed out of her cottage and around to the back. The ground was still muddy from the downpour, but Elizabeth had been right about it only being a short sharp storm. The sky was grey and the smell of damp rose up in my face.

We rounded the corner and saw a large shed, about the size of my garage back home. The big doors were open and inside were about a dozen red quad bikes.

'Cool!' Grace yelled, running over to them.

Quad bikes are like motorcycles with four big wheels. I looked over at them and noticed the seats were bigger than those of a normal motorbike, with a nice wide space to rest your feet. On the handlebars were brakes, just like on my bicycle at home, and some switches.

'This should get us back a little quicker,' Elizabeth smiled warmly.

'Let me on, let me on!' Grace jumped up and down.

'First up: a lesson in quad bike safety,' Elizabeth said, as she pointed her finger in Grace's direction. 'Safety first!'

Grace scrunched up her nose in frustration.

Elizabeth rolled out four smaller quad bikes and lined them up in a row. She told us to sit on one each and began to point out all the features of the bike. She showed us where the 'on' switch was, and told us how to use the 'cut-off' switch in case of an emergency.

Butterflies flittered around my stomach. I exchanged a shy glance with Saskia, who also looked a little out of her comfort zone. Mercedes seemed pretty calm and Grace just couldn't wait to get out on the open road.

Elizabeth showed us how to use the hand throttle, which is how you make the quad bike move. By gently squeezing it, the quad bike would accelerate. The hand brakes were just like those on a bicycle and I felt comfortable manoeuvring my hand onto the brake and gently squeezing it like I would on my bike at home.

'How fast can we go?' Grace blurted, bouncing up and down on the seat of her quad bike.

'These quad bikes are used for tours that I lead around the national park. That's why I have so many of them. But because we have kids using them, they are all fitted with a throttle restrictor. So the answer is, not *too* fast,' Elizabeth smiled.

'Phooey,' Grace mumbled.

'But don't worry, I'm sure you will think it's fast enough!' Elizabeth said. 'Trust me—this is no baby ride at the amusement park!'

We all hopped off the quad bikes and Elizabeth handed out protective gear. We were already wearing long hiking pants and boots, but she handed us a chest and neck protector each, goggles, gloves and, of course, a big motorcycle helmet. We all giggled as we put the chunky headgear on. Mercedes' blue eyes sparkled with excitement.

'I've never done anything like this before!' she breathed a little nervously.

'To start, let's do some gentle riding around this area in little circles,' Elizabeth said, pointing to the wide dirt area around the barn.

We all hopped on our bikes and turned the keys. Then we pressed the buttons to start the ignition. My bike roared to life and my stomach flipped in anticipation. I gently squeezed the throttle and my bike lurched forward.

'Easy does it,' Elizabeth cautioned.

Grace led the way as we formed into single file and rode slowly around the barn.

'Now just a little quicker,' Elizabeth said.

I closed my fingers around the throttle and gently pressed. The quad bike did a little bunny hop underneath me, jerking along. But then it was smooth sailing.

'Woohoo!' Grace squealed as she raced around the barn, the three of us following her.

Elizabeth waved us back over.

'Great job!' she said, beaming.

'How are we going to ride with our packs?' I asked,

suddenly worried about what it would be like to ride with a heavy weight on my back. Our packs were still inside Elizabeth's house.

'Don't you worry about that,' Elizabeth said, walking into the barn. She pulled a helmet over her head, hopped on her own quad bike and rode it out into the open. Attached to the back was a small trailer, which the bike pulled along. 'We'll fit them all in here,' she said, nodding at the trailer.

'I can't believe how lucky we are!' Saskia said. 'Nobody else gets to ride quad bikes on camp!'

'This should save us a lot of time. The quad bike trail is very direct and will get us to the base camp in no time at all. Everyone ready?' Elizabeth said.

We all nodded eagerly.

After loading up our packs and, much to Grace's despair, quickly going over the safety procedures again, we were ready to go!

Elizabeth led the way on her quad bike, with the trailer. She was followed by Grace, then me, then Mercedes, with Saskia bringing up the rear. We rode slowly away from the barn and down a narrow trail. I held my breath as we descended a steep track, worried that my quad bike would go tumbling down the hill. But the bikes were sturdy and we soon reached the wide flat trail.

'Ready to go faster?' Elizabeth called.

'Yahooo!' Grace yelled in response.

The quad bike trail was much wider than the bushwalking trail and allowed us to ramp up the speed. My confidence grew as we flew along, my braid flicking out behind me from under my helmet.

'This is the best thing ever!' Mercedes yelled.

The trail started to incline upwards and I increased the pressure on the throttle to get up the hill.

'What goes up must come down!' Elizabeth sang from the front.

Sure enough, the hill's incline peaked and suddenly we were hurtling downhill at a great speed. The cool air whipped about my face. I was smiling so hard that my cheeks began to sting.

Nanna Kate always loved to tell me about her

adventures. One time, she went horseback riding through the Snowy Mountains. She said nothing in the world compared to racing through the bushland on that horse. She said the freedom she felt, the scent of nature and the thrill of the ride was unlike anything else. And while I wasn't on a horse, I now completely understood what she meant.

Looking ahead, I could see Elizabeth waving her arm in a downward motion, which she had previously told us meant that she wanted us to slow down. We used our brakes to come to a stop and Elizabeth turned around with her finger to her lips in front of her helmet. She signalled for us to hop off our bikes and quietly come over to her. I stepped off my bike and pulled my helmet off. Saskia, Grace, Mercedes and I gathered around Elizabeth, where she was looking high up into the trees.

'There!' she whispered.

We all looked where she was pointing, and sleeping in the fork of a tree was a koala with its baby.

'Oh, it's so cute!' Saskia gushed.

'Every time I see a koala, it's asleep,' Grace said.

'A bit like you on the weekend,' I joked, nudging her.

'How many hours a day do you think they sleep? Guess!' Elizabeth said.

'12?' I ventured.

'15,' Grace said.

'10?' Saskia asked.

'It's, like, 22 hours. I read about it once,' Mercedes said confidently.

Saskia laughed. '22 hours? Mercedes, there are only 24 hours in a day! How can it sleep 22 of them?'

Mercedes frowned.

'Actually Mercedes is right,' Elizabeth said. 'Koalas sleep 18 to 22 hours every day.'

Mercedes looked at us with bright eyes that shimmered with pride. 'See? Not so dumb after all,' Mercedes said, her eyebrows raised.

'Sorry, Mercedes,' Saskia mumbled. 'And I'm sorry about everything, not just that. I'm sorry for what I said before about you being an airhead. You're not an airhead. You're smart and funny and a good friend.'

Mercedes' face softened and she smiled forgivingly

at Saskia. Saskia gave her a small smile back.

'Come on then, let's get back on the road!' Elizabeth said, pulling her helmet back on over her long silvery hair.

We secured our helmets, jumped back onto our quad bikes and raced through the bush. Grace sang loudly over the top of the roar of the bikes and we laughed as we shot through the national park. I breathed in deeply, savouring the feeling as we raced along. And just for a moment, I never wanted that feeling to end.

Chapter 18

As we pulled into the base camp, I felt like a rock star. Everyone had heard us approaching on our quad bikes and one girl screamed, 'Look! There they are!'

Our entire year came running over to us as we slowed to a stop on the bikes.

'Woah, you're so lucky!'

'Quad biking? How cool!'

'How fast did you go?'

'Where did you sleep last night?'

The questions came firing at us at speed and I felt a little overwhelmed.

‘Clear the way and let these girls get off the bikes,’ Elizabeth said, waving her hands for the crowd to disperse.

The other girls began to walk away, but two came running over.

‘Ella! Grace! Are you OK?’

It was Zoe and Violet. They didn’t care about the quad bikes or anything else. They just wanted to know that we were safe and sound.

‘We heard you got lost!’ Violet gasped. ‘Were you on your own for long? We were so worried!’

‘Monty told us one of the national park rangers found you—thank goodness for that!’ Zoe said.

Grace and I hugged our friends. It felt so good to be back with them after our adventure in the wild. But our hugs didn’t last long before we noticed two tall figures waiting behind them. Coach Bright and Ms Montgomery. And they did not look impressed at all.

‘Violet and Zoe, go back to the camping area, please,’ Ms Montgomery said flatly. ‘Girls, come here.’ She beckoned the four of us over.

Saskia, Mercedes, Grace and I shuffled over meekly. Elizabeth walked with us.

'What on earth happened?' Coach Bright bellowed.

'Mercedes got stuck on a ledge when we were going to the toilet at the lookout. By the time we got back, everyone had gone,' Grace said quietly.

'But what I can't understand is why you weren't noticed as missing. We had checklists of names for each group . . .' Ms Montgomery said, shaking her head.

We all stood in awkward silence.

'It was my fault,' Saskia said finally. 'I took our names off the lists so we could switch groups. I never meant for us to get lost though.'

Ms Montgomery's face reddened. 'I knew there was something fishy going on here,' she said. 'What you did was very irresponsible, Saskia.'

'It was me too,' Mercedes said, linking her arm into Saskia's. 'I agreed with her plan.'

'And I rubbed my own name off the list,' I said. I winced at my confession. I knew this was going to get me into more trouble, but I couldn't bear Saskia taking all the blame when I had played my part.

'But I rubbed Grace's name off,' Saskia added. 'Grace did nothing wrong.'

Ms Montgomery nodded. 'Well, thank you for your honesty, girls. There will be repercussions for your actions, but for now,' she said, her face softening slightly, 'I'm so glad you are all safe.'

'It's lucky Elizabeth found you,' Coach Bright added. 'At least we knew you were in the safest of hands.'

Elizabeth smiled. 'You've got some pretty resourceful young ladies here.'

Elizabeth walked away with Coach Bright and Ms Montgomery, filling them in on our grand adventure.

'I can't believe we made it back in one piece.' Grace sighed wistfully.

'Well, it really was true teamwork,' I added, linking arms with her. Mercedes came over and linked arms with me too. Then Saskia joined in on Mercedes' other arm.

'I wish we could do it all again,' Grace said.

Saskia, Mercedes and I exchanged glances.

'Not before a nice long hot shower!' Mercedes laughed.

We all giggled together and walked over to join the rest of our year group.

Chapter 19

× –

From: Ella

Sent: Friday, 8:07 PM

To: Olivia

Subject: I'm baaaaack!

Hi Olivia!

We're back! I can't believe so much happened in the three days we were away at camp. I suppose you heard a bit about our adventure this morning when Ms Montgomery rang Mum and Dad about us getting lost. We were in sooooo much trouble. We have had our weekend privileges revoked for a month and have to do extra kitchen duty. But Mrs Sinclair said even though we did a terrible thing, which led to us getting lost, she was very proud of the teamwork we demonstrated in working together to get back to our group.

Another good thing to come out of our adventure is that the Eden Press article that I'm going to write about our survival in the bush, from my diary notes, will be EPIC! I'm going to include tips on making a raft, lighting a fire without matches, identifying a snake (with Mercedes' help), orienteering and even quad biking! And I bet everyone will love the part about the legend of the Mount Midnight witch. I interviewed Elizabeth before we left and she gave me a whole lot of expert advice on what to do if you get lost in the wild.

It's funny how so much can change in just a short amount of time. We were only alone for one night in the bush, but I feel like a whole new person. I feel like I accomplished so much out there, and all without the security of my BFF. You know Zoe and I have done everything together over the years, but this time I was really brave *without* her. And it felt kinda good.

Mercedes learned that she's smart in her own way. And Saskia has learned to respect her friend a bit more. I noticed on the bus trip back to school that Saskia was already talking to Mercedes with a whole lot more respect. I even heard Saskia ask Mercedes a question about wildlife!

You know how Nanna Kate talks about growing up as being like a big adventure? That's kinda how I feel right now. Like, I went on this camp one way, but have come home different—a little more grown up. Sounds weird, but it's true.

Let's video call tomorrow and I'll tell you more. I can't wait to see your face!

Better go—the line for the showers is insane!

Love,

Ella

xx

Ever since she learnt to hold a pen, Laura Sieveking has loved creating stories. She remembers hiding in her room as a six-year-old, writing a series of books about an unlikely friendship between a princess and a bear.

As an adult, Laura has spent the vast majority of her career working in publishing as an editor. After several years, she decided to put down her red pen and open up her laptop to create books of her own.

Laura's books revolve around all the things she loved as a child—friendships, sport and a little bit of magic. She has written series for early independent readers and middle grade fiction.

She lives in Sydney with her husband and two children, and her fluffy dog who looks like a teddy bear.

Read all the Ella at Eden adventures: